for Jessie
Woolverton

Joyce Warren

THE
UNDERGROUND
BANQUET and other stories

BY JOYCE WARREN

Rowan Tree Press, 124 Chestnut St., Boston, MA 02108

Library of Congress No. 87-063475
ISBN 0-937672-23-8
© 1988 Joyce Warren
Printed in the United States of America

ACKNOWLEDGMENTS

Photograph by Diana Walker
Cover design by Lazarillo
Crash, Time Lucy Went, Mrs. Rogers and *Erika* were first published in
THE NEW YORKER; *Hill Climbing by Boat,* in HARPER'S MAGA-
ZINE; *Mr. McAlligator* and *Mr. Dnarley's Pigs,* in VOGUE.

Rowan Tree Press, 124 Chestnut St., Boston, MA 02108

Dedicated to Jack Robbie, John Andrew, and in memory of Peter

TABLE OF CONTENTS

Crash

I didn't read about the crash in the newspapers, because for awhile I wasn't reading anything, but I was told later that there had been a picture on the front page of the *Washington Post*. I don't usually pay much attention to stories about smashed-up cars, but, of course, it makes a difference if the car and some of the blood splashed on it are your own.

As automobile accidents go, ours wasn't anything out of the ordinary. My husband and I and our two corgis were driving north on a two-lane highway toward Washington, where we live. A driver en route from one Maryland bar to another was travelling south, and he pulled into our lane to pass another car. I saw his car coming, and I remember feeling very much surprised. I wondered what on earth had persuaded him that he had room enough to get by. I didn't arrive at any conclusion—not because I wasn't curious but because I had judged correctly: he didn't have enough room.

I am not a good driver myself. Although I am no longer a young woman, strange men are still apt to drop whatever they may be doing when they see me attempt to park, in order to shout, wave, and offer me the benefit of their technical assistance. I am even worse as a passenger. Every time I pack a basket for a motoring picnic, I have a feeling that I ought to add something for Death to gnaw on, since he will certainly be with us, and probably hungry. I realize that my attitude toward the sport of road travel is a morbid one, and that as a naturalized citizen of the United States (I was born in England) I ought to develop a healthier outlook, but frightened of other drivers is what, when I am in a car, I am.

I have made some progress, nevertheless. I used to speculate, as I made my nervous way along the vast highways that surround Washington, on what I would do if one of the cars approaching me chose to move into my lane. The line of worried reasoning I pursued was the same that I followed years ago during World War II, when I lived in London and the air raids were in full bloom. Then I wondered what I would do if I suddenly found myself buried under a pile of rubble. I wanted very much to emulate the heroes of history and do the right thing instantaneously, without giving the matter a thought, and what bothered me was not so much the prospect of being buried as that in the confusion of the burial I might not have the remotest notion of what *was* the right thing to do. I never found the answer to my rubble question, because the nearest I came to an enemy bomb was the outer edge of its draft, but I have solved the one about the head-on crash. I now know what one does, and although it may sound eccentric to say so, the experience of our crash has consoled me.

The accident happened one wet Saturday evening in September when my husband and I were on our way home after spending a day in the country. Charles was driving, I was in the seat beside him, and the two dogs, an empty picnic hamper, and a load of gardening tools were in back. Our day had gone well; it had been warm and sunny all afternoon, and now, after dark, a light rain was falling. We were taking the trip slowly—we had nothing to do with the evening except get home and give the dogs their suppers, and for once while travelling along a highway I was not thinking about death. What I *was* thinking about was the selfish pleasure of our isolation (for the duration of our drive, no one could reach us, speak with us, or interrupt us), and of how apt one is to associate happiness with the past—things over and done with—instead of with the dailinesses of now. I felt wrapped in a tight cocoon of contentment, and the fact that this was woven chiefly of fresh air and a good dinner did not make it seem any less poetic.

The drive was very familiar. We came down this highway and back up it most weekends, although not always on the same days or at the same hours. We knew the scenery so well that when an "X" that had been missing for months from a TEXACO sign was replaced, we discussed the possible significance of the change. Did it mean that the business—scruffy-looking—had been bought by some ambitious, tidy-up fellow, or that there had been a general over-all improvement in the X trade? On the night of the accident, however, through the blur of the soft rain, everything outside the car was as I expected it to be, and everything inside, too, including a just perceptible anxiety on the part of the younger dog. Her dinner would be late again. Nobody likes it when his gods let him down, and from her earliest years this animal had never wholeheartedly embraced the theory that those who share in family outings must take the rough with the rough.

There was very little traffic going toward Washington, but a fairly steady belt of headlights was coming out. I wondered vaguely whether the cars might be on their way home from Rosecroft Raceway—I had no idea what time of day or night the races there ended. And then suddenly one pair of lights pulled into our lane, and in what must have been a matter of seconds the younger dog (the punctual one) was dead.

The three people involved in the crash owed their lives to using and not using seat belts. My husband and I used them and had ours buckled, and so we were prevented from flying through our windshield. The man driving the other car either did not have a belt or did not have it buckled; when his car burst into flames, he was thrown clear of his own bonfire. I believe the only injury he suffered was a bump on the head and a fright, but our subsequent acquaintance hasn't been the sort that flowers readily into an exchange of confidences and I may be wrong about the fright.

Charles and I collected a string of problems that included a jaw smashed in several different places for him, and a cracked skull for me. At the time, I was puzzled by what had happened but was not in pain from it. I thought I must be dreaming. A part of our car was on fire, and there was an unpleasant odor of burned hair and dung: the dead dog. Off to one side, I could see an oblong block of leaping red and orange flames: the other car. So one *can* dream in color, I thought— not only in black-and-white, as I had supposed. I closed my eyes, as one does when waiting for a nightmare to pass, but when in a while I opened them again the view was the same, although the smell had become stronger. I seemed to be enclosed in some sort of stiff casing that prevented movement—a box, I decided, with a hole cut in it for my face. There seemed no point in trying to get out of the box until I knew how much energy I had, and whether getting out was the best way to expend it. If I wait, I thought, I shall probably discover where I am and what is going on.

It was about then that I learned the answer to my question of what you do when you are involved in a head-on automobile crash. It is nothing, because nothing is called for. At the moment after impact, before policemen, emergency squads, and, finally, doctors and nurses come to your rescue, you are picked up and cared for by a great many people who do not yet know that you have been hurt. I do not understand how this works, and I didn't then, although it seemed sensible enough at the time. Tomorrow, all our friends would hear what had happened to us, but it was tonight that we needed their help. I suppose that since today's thinking could affect tomorrow's behavior, the reverse might occasionally be true, too.

I heard my husband telling someone our name. (Later, when he regained consciousness in hospital, he did not remember helping to lift me out of the smashed car, or even having been in an accident at all.) I was moved from the box and placed on the ground at the side of the road, but I thought it was into an enormous, very comfortable bed. I felt warm, safe, cared for, and pleasantly sleepy, although I was aware of a lot of fuss and noise going on somewhere beyond the end of my bed. A woman's voice assured me over and over that I was going to be all right, and a man cried wildly, "My God, what a mess!" I tried to rouse myself enough to tell them both not to worry; I was sure that, mess or not, I could manage. I wanted to explain that there were limitless supplies of strength and cheerfulness stuffed into the mattress underneath me, and although these were not mine, for the time being they were completely at my disposal. However, when I tried to talk I found I couldn't. So I dozed, and enjoyed my bed.

It was not until I was in the ambulance that I found myself in difficulties. Somehow, in the confusion of moving, my bed seemed to have been left behind, and without it I couldn't breathe properly. Above the scream of the siren, I could hear the ambulance driver and the attendant discussing baseball—they had to shout to make themselves heard. I tried to call out to tell them about my bed and my breathing, but since I couldn't make any sound, I couldn't attract their attention. I felt very much put out. Every breath I took meant lowering a heavy bucket into a deep well and drawing it up again, and both manoeuvers were extremely painful. I decided I would continue breathing until we reached the hospital, and not a moment longer. Once there, since the ambulance men had caused my troubles by leaving my bed behind, they would have to cope with my bucket themselves.

It took me a week to relearn how to breathe, and after that I had to learn how to operate my body. Once, years before, I had been allowed to take the wheel of a transatlantic liner for a few minutes, and what fascinated me most was the time lag between the issue of my instructions to the ship and the ship's response. My post-accident body seemed to work the same way, but less efficiently, and making sure that it carried out my orders was quite tiring. Sometimes it would refuse altogether, particularly at meals. I would spoon soup into my mouth, only to have it run out through a hole that had been made in my throat to enable me to breathe more easily. The soup would then reassemble itself in a piping-hot puddle on my bosom. This was not only uncomfortable, but also, to my mind, wasted effort, but when in a light moment I wrote a note to the nurse—I was unable to talk—suggesting that I cut out a stage in the proceedings by pouring the soup directly onto my night clothes, she could not read my writing, and merely scowled.

Charles and I were in the same hospital, and from time to time reports were brought to me about his progress. One day, a nurse wheeled him into my room. My husband looked thin and tired and badly knocked about, but he reached his hands out eagerly, and I ordered my hands to do the same. They obeyed at once, and seeing them behave so well gave me the idea that it would be a great relief if I could cry. I tried to think what instructions I should give myself to produce tears, but I did not know, and so I took up my scratch pad instead. I intended to ask Charles if he was still in pain, if he could eat and sleep now, and if, at the time of the crash, he had prayed for us both or whether, like me, he had been so full of astonishment and curiosity and the pleasures of *his* bed that he had forgotten.

But before I started to write, Charles said, "Don't try to talk. We shall have years."

So until the nurse wheeled him away, we sat in silence with our hands touching gently—too dry to weep, and too weak to hold, but contented enough, I think.

Fetters

She was tiny, ancient, sparkling, and as resilient as a pocket-sized trampoline. One could describe her as good only if good were not used in a pejorative sense. She had the knack of making men feel protective and women confiding, and both groups treated her with the kind of respect they might accord a duchess who had escaped from the pages of a European fairy tale. As for children and dogs, they behaved as if she were one of themselves—an instant co-conspirator. She was sweet and brave and easily taken in ("He picked this corn this morning. He told me so."), and she believed the best of people because the worst seemed to her to lack elegance. ("Their relationship is platonic. It must be. She goes driving with him with her hair in curlers.") Her name was Frances Leigh, and wherever she went she left behind her an uplift of the spirit and some twinges of resentment. If one invited Frances to a party, the party was bound to be a success. On the other hand, all the compliments would be propelled in her direction, and no other woman would be given so many chances to take the floor with the best dancer in town.

Frances was not one to hide her light under a bushel: she worked to make herself attractive. This was the reason for those resentful twinges—her contemporaries could more easily have stomached her popularity if her charm had been naturally born, like her large, very soft, brown eyes. But her cultivated enthusiasm for other people's interests was so tactfully expressed that the objects of it seldom spotted her duplicity. I am not even sure that duplicity is the right word for her sudden bursts of excitement over hydroponic gardening, surface friction between metals, or Nathan Milstein's playing. It was an attitude that time couldn't dampen. Frances was 84 when she died, and the day before her passing she went out to tea. "I'm afraid we were mostly old women," she admitted to me on her return, "but there was one very nice retired General who sat next to me and told me all about the Philippines."

I was Frances Leigh's only child, and of course I took her behavior for granted, although I was vaguely aware that other children's mothers were more predictable than mine. She once jumped out of a fourth-floor window because a man who was installing a new fire-escape system in the building suggested that she try it out. Frances shot to the ground inside a long canvas tube and emerged safely at the bottom, only to learn that the installer had thrown a fit. He had meant to be joking.

Although no child, nor for that matter anyone else, could be bored in her company, she had very little imagination. She sincerely believed that life has few problems if one remains cheerful and observes the rules. By rules, she meant the behavior proper to one's position in society, or, as the Church of England Catechism expresses it, "Doing my duty in that state of life to which it shall please God to call me."

I was educated, as my mother was not, to question everything, including social mores, and the result was that she and I argued a great deal. I thought her fettered, and she thought me adrift. I was appalled by the lack of opportunity offered her as a girl to pursue a career: she was equally appalled by the idea that marriage and a family might not offer career enough. As for Women's Lib, she laughed at it. She thought it very clever of American women to pretend that they were hardly done by when, according to her, they were the most pampered beings alive.

I wish, now that it is too late, that I had spent more time finding out about my mother's fetters, but when we discussed them I was so busy putting forward my own point of view that I paid very little attention to hers. I should, however, have learned even less than I did about them if it had not been for that automobile accident.

Frances Leigh wasn't a part of the accident, although she reached our hospital almost as soon as we did. Before Charles lost consciousness, he gave her name and telephone number to the Rescue Squad that scraped us up off the Indian Head Highway. My mother was living in a little apartment on Wisconsin Avenue then, about a mile from our George-town house, and when the hospital called her (the message was simply "Come at once"), she had already gone to bed. She got up, put a coat on over her nightdress, and ran out into the street and hailed a taxi. It was late on a Saturday night and the traffic was heavy. The taxi took nearly an hour to cross town and reach our hospital.

The authorities, my mother said afterward, were very kind. They gave her a cup of tea and sat her in a hallway where Charles and I would be wheeled past on our way from surgery. My mother failed to recognize Charles at all, but she knew me, and she told me later that we smiled at each other. After I had been wheeled away, the nurses assured Frances that Charles and I were in excellent hands and she had nothing to worry about. Since (typically) it did not occur to her to doubt the truth of this remark, she returned to her apartment by the way she had come, and slept well during what was left of the night.

For the first few days I was unable to focus: the crack in my skull prevented me from seeing properly beyond the end of my bed. I was aware that shadowy white figures moved back and forth there, but I couldn't distinguish one from another, and I didn't particularly associate any of them with myself. Then, in a while (I don't know how long) my focussing began to improve, and I saw that the white figures were doctors and nurses, and that in among them, smaller than the rest and always wearing a bright color—a red suit, a green hat, or a checked scarf—was Frances. Most of the time she just sat on a chair nearby, but now and again I noticed her resting on the next bed.

Of course I was very pleased to see her. Her presence gave some roots and continuity to my situation, whatever that might be. Charles did not seem to be around, so since I couldn't talk but could move my hands, I wrote my mother a note on the scribbling pad that a thoughtful friend had brought in to be placed near my pillow. She replied matter-of-factly to my enquiry that Charles was comfortably settled in a room of his own on the next floor. She did not explain the reason for this, nor why we had been separated, and I didn't feel up to pressing her. (She added that since the second bed in my room was not needed at the moment, she was using it to take naps.)

Plenty of people have stout-hearted, courageous mothers who recognize that fussing over a disaster does no good, and I do not mean to deny Frances's gallant behavior by saying that it would have been quite impossible for her to behave in any other way than the way she did. The thinking of the era in which she had grown up—Late-Victorian England—was so firmly impressed on her that she couldn't have disowned it. Although in some social circles one was permitted to fall apart when faced with an emergency, in Frances's one was not. Along with certain social privileges went certain responsibilities, one of which was that one did not give way to emotion. She belonged to that stratum about which all the Englishman's stiff-upper-lip jokes are told. Once, during a Royal Air Force display at an airfield near London, one of the aerobatic pilots found himself in trouble. He had the choice of making a forced landing in a small public park dotted with children, or on an electrified railroad. He chose the railroad, where he was killed instantly. Years

later, the pilot's mother told me that the worst part of that day for her—
she was watching the display—was not her son's death but the hysterical
behavior of his French wife. Never having been taught, as the English
family had, to meet disaster with silent, stony faces, the wife shrieked
and then fainted.

The rules my mother lived by were mostly neither written down nor
spoken of, though occasionally people tried. Table manners—the way
in which one held a champagne glass, gripped a knife and fork, or
decapitated a soft-boiled egg—indicated to the initiated to which circle
of society one belonged, as did one's accent and one's choice of words:
Anglo-Saxon roots took precedence over those of the Romance languages, so napkin was all right, serviette was not. During the Eighteenth Century, some effort was made to fill the gap by the publication
of Books of Manners, but these were hardly serious guides for weather-
ing polite society. "A lady never looks well when gnawing a bone," says
one, and another: "Do not finger the food. The practiced eye will soon
discern the largest piece."

With so little to go on—almost nothing written, and very little
said—it was hard for the young to know what was expected of them.
Children watched their parents like hawks. My own worst *gaffe* concerned a street fight that I got into with a village boy. I was ten and he
was eleven, and the reason we fought was that he had taken to shouting
insulting remarks whenever I walked past his house as I had to do on
my way to and from my piano lesson. George was bigger and heavier
than I was, but not as light on his feet, and my attack (I started it) took
him by surprise. I managed to topple him over and sit squarely on his
chest, from which vantage point I took an ear in each hand and banged
his head up and down on the road until it bled. When, later, I reported
my success to my parents, I was astonished to be met with disapproval.
George, they explained, being a village boy, could not be expected to
know better than to shout rude remarks, whereas I was a lady, and

ladies, however seriously provoked, do not bang heads on highways until they bleed.

I wondered what would happen when George and I next met, but something must have been said at his house too, because he stopped speaking to me altogether, unless it is accounted as speaking to stare at the sky and hiss through clenched teeth.

By the time I was growing up, the class structure that had governed my mother's youth had pretty much ceased to exist. Two World Wars helped, of course—a country can hardly conscript women into its wartime labor force and also expect them to creep back into their former lives once peace has been declared. My mother thought that my generation paid dearly for its freedoms, and perhaps we did. "It only makes people dissatisfied to tell them they can do anything with their lives that they want to do if only they work hard enough," she said once. "And it means that the people at the bottom who like it there feel guilty not to be improving themselves."

Put simply, my mother saw it as her role in life to make every man she met feel appreciated and admired. This was not hard for her because she genuinely considered men to be superior beings, and on the rare occasions when she met a man who did not immediately agree with her, she made it her agreeable duty to persuade him to change his mind.

My mother's attitude meant, of course, that she was a devoted and doting wife. I don't think she believed my father capable of a selfish thought or an uncharitable deed, and when (occasionally) appearances belied this, she disbelieved the evidence. I remember expostulating at the way my mother always put the car away if it was raining when she and my father came home from a drive. My father would step straight from the car into our warm entrance hall, and leave my mother to drive on another quarter of a mile or so to the end of a muddy driveway, where she garaged the car in a converted coach-house. I said I couldn't see why my father shouldn't put the car away occasionally when the weather was bad. "Your father doesn't like to get wet," my mother explained.

It was hopeless trying to do what a later generation has called consciousness-raising with her. Once when I thought my father had behaved particularly exasperatingly, I asked my mother what had made her marry him. "He can always make me laugh," she said.

I enjoyed my freedom very much, but I didn't escape altogether from the clutches of an earlier class system. I might not be expected to live by its regulations, but its atmosphere was all around me. One night during World War II, I was alone in a friend's house in London. The Air Raid Warning sounded, and I realized to my relief that since I was alone and nobody could know, I could relax this time and give vent to my fear of the bombers: scream, roll on the floor, tear my hair. I supposed that I would feel much better if I could express myself, but I was wrong. After I had spent the raid weeping and throwing myself about I felt much worse than I did when I behaved. Stiff-upper-lip training had had its effect.

My mother, of course, neither permitted herself, nor seemed to need, such cowardly relaxation. During the V-1 attacks, she and I were sharing a small apartment in central London. The bombs came over at such short intervals that it was hard to find opportunities to shop, cook, eat, or take a bath. An approaching bomb made a put-put sound like a motor-bicycle, and so long as one could hear this, one was all right. But then the bomb's engine would cut off, and there would be about fifteen seconds of silence before it hit the ground and exploded. During that fifteen seconds, one was advised to lie flat on the ground.

One time at the height of the V-1's, I wanted to wash my hair. I asked my mother to listen for the bombs for me, and to tell me if one cut off while I had my head submerged in soapy water. She agreed, and I washed my hair, but as I finished I heard a V-1 explode. "You promised you'd warn me," I said.

"You know, you're getting jumpy," my mother replied. Then she added: "I have no intention of letting Hitler decide when you are or are not to wash your hair."

Frances Leigh was in her seventies when she made the move from England to join me in America. Our friends warned us that she might be homesick, and that I must be prepared to ship her back to England if the adjustment at her age proved too great. I wasn't worried. I was sure that she would settle in quickly, and she did. The novelty of her new country delighted her. ("They're giving those nice friends of yours a *baby shower!* How does it work, I wonder—do you clip it to the side of the bath-tub?" And "Rest Rooms beside the highway—so considerate. Nobody in England ever thinks one might like to lie down and rest during a long drive . . .")

She didn't change her habits, of course. I once heard her assuring a young man at a cocktail party that she was intensely interested in Mayan Art. When I enquired about this later, she looked surprised and said: "But Mayan Art is Dr. Turner's field, and nobody was speaking to him."

Perhaps it was the unreality of our surroundings that made it possible for my mother to talk as freely as she did as we lay side by side in our hospital beds. Or perhaps it was because I couldn't answer her except in writing (it was weeks before I relearned how to speak) and she was eager to keep my mind off my breathing problems and help the hours to pass. Whatever the reason, I learned a lot more than I had known before about the society she had grown up in. She wore her fetters with an air, and it was clear from the way she described her early life that she thoroughly enjoyed the games she played within the restrictions they imposed. There were rules for everything, even conversation. At a formal dinner, for example, a lady spoke first with the man on her left, and then, half way through the meal, she would begin speaking with the man at her right. The timing of this change was up to the hostess, who at a certain convenient point, and under the covert but alert eyes of the other women, would "turn the table." Topics of conversation when ladies were present were controlled by the ladies, who, although they must steer clear of certain taboo subjects—religion was one, politics another—were free to talk about what interested *them*. My mother could handle a gun, ride a horse, drive a car, and fly an airplane, well enough so that she could discuss them sensibly. Primarily, though, the purpose of a dinner was to make an enjoyable occasion for men, and therefore it was the men who were encouraged to do most of the talking. Frances had a story about one dinner partner of hers who talked right through his half of the meal about methods of crop-rotation. Frances said nothing—she wasn't given the chance—but after dinner her partner sought out his hostess to remark on what a brilliant conversationalist Frances was.

As the talks between our hospital beds proceeded, it became clear to my mother and me that each of us felt sorry that the other had missed so much. No amount of talk on Frances's part could convince me that fetters are not still fetters even if there is room to manoeuvre inside them, and no amount of scribbling on a scratch pad could convince Frances that the freedoms I cherished were not dismally lacking in *panache*. When I wrote of equal pay and equal opportunity, she shook her head and assured me that a woman who couldn't get her own way in a man's world without recourse to the law must need her head examined.

Frances came to the hospital faithfully, every afternoon, but in spite of the amount of time we spent communicating with each other, we didn't really cover much ground. I was slow with my scribbling pad, and she, although she tried to be patient, kept one eye on the clock. She always left my room in time to be down in the hospital lobby by five. She had a ride home then with one of my doctors who lived near (well, not very near) her apartment.

Ugly Douglas & Company

It was quite a while before I understood my imprisonment—before I realized that I was trapped inside my own injured body, and that what I could do was governed by what it could do, or was prepared to do. To begin with, I wasn't clear whether I was alive or dead. At the hospital to which my ambulance took me—I'll call it Mockley Memorial—I learned from voices around me that I was not expected to live through the night. The next morning, Dr. Mockley, the man whose memorial the hospital was, came to see me. Since people do not normally work inside their own memorials, I assumed from his visit that both he and I were dead.

But then the conversation got down to so many small, earthly practicalities that I wondered. (I might not be able to speak, but there was nothing wrong with my hearing). Someone apparently wanted to move me from the wilds of Maryland to downtown Washington, D.C., and Dr. Mockley made the point, loudly, that if I were moved I would not survive the journey. This remark comforted me very much. If in talking about my death, he could use the conditional future rather than the past perfect, I must be alive.

I was moved to Washington a week later. The intervening time passed quickly because I had never been a hospital patient before and I had, I found, to do all my own breathing. I would have liked help with this (to me) important work, but there seemed to be nobody at Mockley Memorial to provide it. I therefore stayed on the job myself for eight nights and seven days—not bad going, really, for someone as new to hospital routine as I.

By the time I was moved into town—to Hill Hospital on Sixteenth Street—my breathing had considerably improved, but owing to the shortage of accommodation there, this bed I was allocated had a large hole underneath it. This wouldn't have bothered me except for the fact that the hole went through a glass roof (my bed was on top of the roof) into Liverpool Street railroad station, London. Down below, steam locomotives hissed and snorted, freight cars shunted, whistles blew, doors banged, and every sound echoed.

I was disappointed. I had my own doctor now instead of Dr. Mockley, and I had hoped that he would have been able to find me a more congenial bed. I thought of writing him a note, but then I decided that this would be selfish. I was an emergency case, and obviously if there had been a better bed available (the one next to mine in the two-bedded room was empty, but I could see from the steam that arose from underneath it that it too was over a hole), in a better bed I would be.

There was no mistaking Liverpool Street station. Its sounds and smells were only too familiar. For nine years, I had visited it six times a year on my journeys to and from boarding school. My parents had unfortunately taken the view that because I was an only child, it was good for me to be educated at a large, tough establishment populated by clever, hardy girls. What one learned there was mainly how to survive—both the girls and the weather. The health-giving winds of Norway reached our east coast promontory unimpeded, all year round.

Most of my peers came from homes in or near London, and for their benefit the school chartered a special train. My home was in a remote section of Derbyshire, and I had to take a long cross-country journey before I could join the others at the Liverpool Street terminal. My trip from home to school took thirteen hours, of which the few minutes I spent in Liverpool Street station were the worst.

I am sure that if I had told my parents what a nightmare those occasions were for me, they would have done something about it—arranged for me to go by another route, perhaps, or sent me to a different school. But knowledge is not self-integrating, and although I knew that grappling with Liverpool Street was not the ordeal to the others that it was to me, I assumed that the reason I felt haunted was that I was a born coward.

An aunt always met me and saw me across London, but having taken me to the right platform at Liverpool Street she did not buy a platform ticket for herself so that she could see the train leave. She considered her duty done, and made for home. Usually my connections from Derbyshire were such that I had no time for family reunions; I would have been too fussed to enjoy them anyway. I only remember being early at Liverpool Street once, and then I nearly missed the school train altogether because I had to wait to be rescued by a locksmith from the First-Class Ladies. (I became a Second-Class Lady after that, but never an assured one). The large, dirty, extremely noisy station seemed to me a place of extraordinary hazard. I mislaid luggage, tickets, and tennis racquets, and once a porter disappeared for good with my suitcase. On another occasion, as if looking for trouble, I fell flat on my face trying to avoid a basket of pigeons, and returned to school with torn stockings and blood oozing from both my knees.

The train itself contained its own problems. A rigid caste-system prevailed on board. Important persons such as prefects and games captains occupied the rear; dogs-bodies, the front. Although as time went on I worked my way towards the center portion of the train, I never attained backend status: literature (I once won a prize for that) didn't rate beyond half way. People like myself needed to reach Liverpool

Street early enough to obtain their appropriate status *from the outside:* it was a social *gaffe* of the worst order to do so from within. But time and again, as I skittered along the platform, the train would start to move, and I would be seized by the irate teacher in charge, and bundled in at the nearest door. This would invariably throw me above my station, and as I rectified matters, my face would be scarlet and my embarrassment extreme. And now here I was in hospital, with the whole business bothering me again from under the bed.

I had six broken ribs and a collapsed lung, in addition to my fractured skull, and I had frequently to be wheeled from my room on the fifth floor to the X-Ray Department below, across the entrance hall from the Gift Shop. Children were allowed into the hospital as far as the shop, and one day I saw two little girls there with their mother. I smiled at them, or rather, I intended to smile, but apparently something quite different happened to my face. After startled, horrified glances, the children ran away.

I was making progress, though. I was able to get up by myself, and walk a little in the corridor. There was a sofa there, and a table with a lamp, and when I saw them it occurred to me that I could avoid the night sounds of Liverpool Street by spending my nights there, instead of in bed.

The notion worked very well for a couple of nights. I read and dozed in the quiet, and the night-nurses, most of whom ran homes of their own in the day time, were only too pleased to let me do as I liked so long as I didn't disturb them. Then one night I found someone else sitting on my sofa—a small schoolgirl. She looked, I thought, about ten years old.

She wasn't a pretty child, and her appearance wasn't improved by the way her straight hair was arranged—brushed back from her forehead into two short braids. She wore steel-rimmed spectacles, and she carried a black and white guinea-pig in her arms. His name, she said, was Ugly

Douglas. He was a fine specimen of a pig—white with black splotches, one splotch covering an eye and part of his blunt nose.

I was worried, after my experience with the Gift Shop children, that I might frighten the little girl if I smiled, so I didn't, and beyond moving up to make room for me on the sofa, she took very little notice. Her chief concern was with her pig, who seemed extremely happy. His body sagged in her lap, and with his eyes closed and his nostrils momentarily still, he looked like a small, good-quality handbag, with four clenched feet for clasps.

I slept some, and when I woke up the little girl and the pig had gone. She came again the next night though, and regularly after that. She didn't always bring Ugly Douglas, although he was obviously her favorite. Sometimes a red corgi puppy came, or a pair of white rats. Child and animals were always deeply interested in each other, and this was fine with me. I liked to watch them and be with them, but I didn't want to share their affections, or belong. During the day, I kept meaning to ask the little girl who she was and what she was doing here by herself night after night, but when I saw her, I forgot, and in any case conversation would have been tiresome—I would have had to write a letter.

One day my doctor asked how I was sleeping. I wrote: "I don't sleep. I sit on the sofa outside."

The doctor replied that we must put a stop to that immediately. He prescribed pills, and hot milk at ten. I was appalled. I couldn't think why I had been so foolish as to mention the sofa. Now I would have to stay over Liverpool Street until I was judged well enough to go home.

It wasn't until after I had been home for several weeks, and was well enough to go for walks and to swim again, that it occurred to me that there couldn't really have been a hole under my bed, and that Liverpool Street and its noises must have belonged not with Hill Hospital, but with the crack in my skull.

And then of course I was able to place the little girl, and the animals that I had owned, years before. I needn't, I thought, be ashamed of my cowardice, or embarrassed by the child I had been. (She, apparently, wasn't afraid of the adult she would become.) Somewhere inside me, outside time, this child still was, and in the months of my learning that lay ahead—learning to eat hard food, to climb stairs, to greet people, to talk—she and Ugly Douglas and the others would be there to remind me not to take myself too seriously. It was up to me now, the doctor had said, and I could see that. All the same, it was comforting to remember, as I faced a future that at the moment appeared covered with bumps and traps, that it belonged to the child as well as to me, and that in a sense, therefore, I wouldn't be facing it alone.

Mr. Dnarley's Pigs

At the time of the accident, Charles and I had lived long enough in Washington, D.C., so that when it was known we had settled into Hill Hospital for a fairly long stay, we had a great many callers. I was pleased and touched that so many people came, but I was distressed as well, because I found it hard to separate reality from delusion. I couldn't remember people's names nor their relationships to each other, and although I was aware that I knew them, I didn't always know why. At one period of my recovery I seemed to spend quite a lot of time sitting in the snow on the top of a mountain. It was cold but quite comfortable there except for the bright sunlight that hurt my eyes, and I had no particular wish to move until a geology colleague of Charles's suddenly joined me. She wasn't dressed for our location—she had on a light wool dress and thin shoes—and I reached for my scribbling pad at once and began a note saying that we would go somewhere warmer, but I felt alarmed and almost tearful at seeing her because I didn't know where we could go. Before I had finished writing, however, the problem had answered itself. My friend had left, taking (temporarily) the mountain with her.

Though I found it tiring at the time, I am sure it had therapeutic value for me to have to cope with visitors. I felt compelled to make an effort at conversation by way of my scribbling pad, and not just lie there inert. And every now and again some incident would occur which would serve to attach me more firmly, and for longer periods, to reality. There was, for example, the orange.

The orange was a present: a large, glowing, California navel. The moment I saw it I thought of another, large, glowing California navel which Charles had produced from his brief case one night when I dined with him in London during World War II. It was the first orange I had seen for several months (orange *juice* was available on children's ration books, but not even that on those issued to adults), and the idea of simply taking my orange home and eating it, as Charles expected me to do, was out of the question. Oranges were no more indigenous to my wartime manner of living than were yachts, suits of sables, or private airplanes.

After keeping my present for a day or two and trying without success to make its donor share it with me, I invited some children in. (This was more difficult than it may sound because most London children had either been evacuated to the country or shipped to North America for the duration). Eventually, however, I unearthed four boys who for various reasons had already been restored to their mothers. Together, the five of us opened my treasure and counted its pigs (an English term for fruit sections). Satisfactorily, there were ten of them. Two apiece.

I don't suppose that that link in my head between the two navel oranges would have been strong enough to give me the forceful tug back into reality that it did if it hadn't reminded me of Mr. Dnarley. That was the name that he (or someone) wrote on a piece of cardboard and left leaning against a stack of *Washington Posts* one morning—GONE FOR CHANGE DNARLEY.

Mr. Dnarley operates a news pile—one cannot call it a stand—on what must be one of the most weather-beaten corners in Washington, D.C. His wares are stacked in a shallow recess in the side of a bank building, and he squats alongside them. The recess gives the papers and magazines some shelter, and it prevents passers-by from treading on Mr. Dnarley, but it gives him little protection from the wind, the sun, the cold, and the ceaseless racket of heavy traffic.

For ten hours a day, every day except Sundays, Thanksgiving, and Christmas, Mr. Dnarley operates his store. He is a large man, solid, tall and broad, with a heavy, loaf-shaped face, red leathery skin, and small, very alert black eyes. Winters, he sits wrapped in several layers of coats and sweaters, wearing stout boots, heavy socks, knitted gloves with a hole or two in them, and a knitted cap with snug earpieces. Summers, he changes to patched cotton trousers, a T-shirt out of which burst brawny arms tattooed with anchors, and a straw hat with a small brim. I do not know which season of the year he prefers: it must all be profoundly uncomfortable.

Mr. Dnarley almost never speaks, but his observation of life about him is sharp: I am sure he doesn't miss a thing. From his behavior over the years to me, I think he does not like women. For months I used to wish him good day when I passed, but as he never acknowledged my greeting I gave up. One time, when I offered him the wrong money for a magazine I was buying, he slammed the coins back into my hand and waited in silence for me to figure out my mistake, instead of explaining what was wrong, as anyone else would have done.

To begin with, I thought his churlishness might be associated with my dogs. We make a somewhat disorganized party as we lurch along with our shopping, library books, and leashes, but we are always a friendly one, and the dogs perfectly well understand the difference between newspapers on the floor and newspapers on the floor for sale.

But Mr. Dnarley was no more affable in his dealings with my husband, who stops at the pile every evening on his way home from work.

Of course the noise and the crowds there do not encourage conversation, but one would suppose that a nod of recognition might not be considered effusive in the case of a long-term, regular customer.

We grow roses in our small Washington garden, and so far we have always had some to pick for Thanksgiving. One year, our flowers did particularly well, and on the Wednesday of Thanksgiving week my husband took a bunch to his office to give away. He put the best Peace rose in water and saved it till evening, and on his way home he presented it to Mr. Dnarley with his good wishes, telling him to take it home to his girl. Mr. Dnarley looked baffled, but after a moment's pause, he took the flower. Then, without changing the expression of his eyes, my husband said, he bent the corners of his mouth upward, as one might the sides of a music stand. Mr. Dnarley was smiling.

The Friday after Thanksgiving was a cold day that year, and my husband was startled to see that Mr. Dnarley wasn't tending his pile. A boy was selling instead, and taking so much time over the job that my husband did not like to delay him further by asking where Mr. Dnarley was.

We worried about him all that weekend. We wondered whether our rose had gone to Mr. Dnarley's head: maybe he had left us for good and gone to Baltimore and sailed away in a freighter. Or perhaps he had arrived very early at his place of business to put things into fresh order after the holiday, and frozen solid at his post. We pictured him dying in one of the city's hospitals, without so much as thawing out. But on Monday my husband telephoned from the office to say Mr. Dnarley was back, looking rugged, sharp-eyed, and surly as usual.

That evening, my husband, taking advantage, as a man will, of a relationship that has progressed to the flower-giving stage, told Mr. Dnarley when he bought his paper that he was pleased to see him, and that he hoped his absence on Friday had not been because he was sick. To his astonishment, Mr. Dnarley answered. In a cracked, piping voice, gentle for so large a man, that had a note of amazement in it as if he had just survived an experience he hoped never to repeat, Mr. Dnarley said: "Took the day off, that's all. First time in twenty-five years."

When Charles told me about this, I remembered my orange, and I thought that perhaps I knew what Mr. Dnarley had just been through. My gift had seemed so munificent, so lavish, so impossibly beyond my station in life, that I wasn't really able to enjoy it: I was afraid I wouldn't treat it right.

Mr. Dnarley, driven by our rose, or perhaps by weeks of planning, to take the plunge and absent himself from his horrid niche for ten whole hours, had not known, when the time actually came, how to treat that right either.

To use the hours for sleep would have been cowardly, to take a bus or train too expensive or too adventurous; to walk perhaps too strange; and yet to stay at home and let the leisure run through his fingers might be miserly, even gluttonous. Mr. Dnarley had, I thought, been worse off with his ten pigs than I had with mine. Orange sections can be shared. Hours can't. There wouldn't have been anyone Mr. Dnarley could invite in to help him consume his bonus, because we've already got all of it that we're allowed: twenty-four hours a day apiece. All of us, especially all children, already *have* time.

Mrs. Rogers

My struggles dragged on—first the effort to differentiate between reality and delusion, and then the effort to separate the present from the past. Something would happen in the hospital which would remind me of a similar event in my memory, and off I would go, as I had with the orange, thinking about people and incidents that hadn't crossed my mind for years. Mrs. Lewis Rogers, for example. When she moved into the next bed (she had come in to have a cartilage removed from her knee), I was reminded of another Mrs. Lewis Rogers I had known when I was a student. The two of them could hardly have had less in common—apart, of course, from their names—for my earlier Mrs. Lewis Rogers was the only woman I have ever known who played Noel Coward music on the bells of a London church. She played it regularly, sending "Bitter Sweet," "This Year of Grace," "On with the Dance" and "Cavalcade" floating out several days a week over the lunch-hour traffic.

Mrs. Rogers's husband, Dr. Rogers, was rector of a church I will call St. Agnes. He was one of the best-known preachers in England in the late nineteen-thirties. My father and Dr. Rogers were at Cambridge together, and both became Church of England ministers—Dr. Rogers with a city pastorate and my father with a country one. The two men saw little of each other after they left the university, but they kept in touch, and when I went to London as a student, my father sent Dr. Rogers my address. I had a room in a women's hostel, and soon after I had settled in, I got a letter from Mrs. Rogers inviting me to Sunday afternoon tea.

I had heard about the Rogerses all my life, but until that tea I had never met them. I knew what Dr. Rogers looked like from his pictures in the newspapers (he was tall, and—for a middle-aged man—handsome, I thought), and I had heard his powerful voice over the radio making charitable appeals. My father said that he was one of those people who seem to know from the first what they want to do in life. Lewis Rogers had gone directly from Cambridge to a theological college. Afterward, he had worked in a seamen's mission in Liverpool and then in a fashionable London suburb before going to his charge at St. Agnes.

There are eight theatres in St. Agnes parish, and in one of these Dr. Rogers met his wife—met Alice. She was playing the piano in a revue, and a great many people—Alice herself among them—objected to the idea of his marrying her. She pointed out that she had neither the education nor the interest in religion that the wife of the rector of St. Agnes ought to have. Dr. Rogers replied that he did not care a button about her education, and as for her lack of interest in religion, that might not be a bad thing in the wife of a preacher.

My parents' opinion was that in marrying Alice Dr. Rogers showed very good sense. Alice might not have had much formal education, but she came from a close-knit family (her father, two of her uncles, and her brother were on the stage, and a grandfather had been a famous clown), and she had the cheerfulness and adaptability that her new life called for. She was younger than her husband by a good many years, but this did not, as some people said it would, send her running back into the theatre once the novelty of the St. Agnes rectory wore off. "She's a charming woman," my mother told me before I went to London, "And when you meet her, notice her hair—how beautifully brushed it is."

When I went to that first tea at the Rogerses', they had been married about ten years. The St. Agnes rectory enchanted me at once, in a way no other house has ever done. Part of the reason was simply its location. It stood on a small rise between two busy thoroughfares, one running northeast and the other northwest, that converged and joined in front of it. It was a tall, angular house, and its bay-windowed front jutted out into the traffic like a ship with a rounded prow. It was Georgian, built of stone, and coated with soot. I arrived at four o'clock, to find a tea party already going on. Some fifteen or twenty people, most of them near my own age, were standing about the rectory living room with teacups in their hands. There were plates of cakes and sandwiches and a bowl of buttered crumpets on a round table in the bay window. Mrs. Rogers came forward to greet me—a short, slim woman with a serene face and gleaming red hair, and I saw what my mother had meant about brushing. Mrs. Rogers shook hands with me warmly and introduced me to the other people in the room. Many of them were actors, or student actors from London theatre schools. One guest was a girl who was studying fashion drawing, and another was a Jamaican doctor, somewhat older than the rest of us. As the cakes and crumpets disappeared, a woman in a white apron brought in fresh ones. Mrs. Rogers introduced me to her, too. She was the housekeeper, Mrs. Tucker.

The room was large enough so it didn't seem crowded, and as comfortably shabby as our own living room at home. There were built-in bookcases full of books with the titles rubbed and worn, some hunting prints, and an oil painting of a young man in a satin waistcoat. On a stand at one side of the window there was a large bird cage containing a fat canary whose name, the Jamaican told me, was Noah. Noah's cage was equipped with all kinds of swings, seesaws, parallel bars, and other sporting gear, but he seemed to have given up on his figure, and instead of exercising he preferred to loll on a small bench conveniently placed where he could see his reflection in a small oval mirror.

Presently, Dr. Rogers came in, looking exactly like his pictures. He bowed in the general direction of the cake table, and then went to the opposite end of the room and sat down in a large armchair. Immediately, Mrs. Tucker appeared carrying a tray on which were arranged a small pot of tea, a milk jug, a sugar bowl, and a plate of *petits-beurres.* She set the tray down beside the rector, and Mrs. Rogers drew a stool up next to him and poured.

For ten minutes or so, there were two distinct tea parties in the room—The Rogerses' and the Rogerses' guests'. When Dr. Rogers was on his second cup, Mrs. Rogers came to our end of the room and selected a couple of us to present to her husband. As a newcomer, and the daughter of an old friend, I was one. Dr. Rogers shook hands with me and inquired kindly about my father. He asked, "How many of you are there? I'm afraid I forget."

"Just me," I said.

He looked me over doubtfully. "Few and fit," he muttered. "Ah, well. . . ."

That was about as much conversation as I ever had with Dr. Rogers at any one time, although after my first visit I often went to tea at the rectory on Sunday afternoons; Mrs. Rogers gave me an open invitation, and it was a pleasant habit to get into. I thought it very nice of her to make time to entertain much the same young group week after week when she led such a crowded social life in addition. Judging from the array of invitation cards on the living-room mantelpiece, the Rogerses attended a great many parties. One day, I discovered that about half the cards were old ones. Mrs. Rogers explained that she kept them after the parties were over because they made such good scrapers for the floor of

Noah's cage. "The Lord Mayor's are the best," she said. "They're very thick, with a sloping gilt edge."

I had been going to Mrs. Rogers' teas for several months before it dawned on me why the other guests and I were invited. We constituted one of her wedges. Dr. Rogers worked all the time among disappointed, disillusioned, dissatisfied people who came to St. Agnes from all over the British Isles. They waited in line for hours to hear him preach, and even longer in the waiting room outside his office to consult him privately about their problems. Dr. Rogers was supposed to take Mondays off, but I don't think he often did. He loved his work, and he was extremely good at it. But he didn't have any hobbies, or any children. He had nothing whatever to distract him from his calling, except his wife. Once, Mrs. Rogers asked me, "You know what it feels like to be lazy, don't you?"

"Well, yes," I said. "Everyone does."

"Not Lewis," she said. "He hasn't any idea. And, you know, if a person has to *ask* what's attractive about sloth, there's really no way to explain." She was laughing at him, but at the same time she was concerned. "He's much the same about leisure. The only reason we go to the theatre as much as we do is to please me, and because his doctor says he must have *some* relaxation."

"But it was in a theatre that he met you."

"Yes, but he hadn't come to see the show. He'd come to meet his parishioners."

So Mrs. Rogers dedicated herself to inserting wedges of entertainment into her husband's schedule, and, up to a point, she was just as successful at her job as he was at his. I don't know how many wedges she thought up altogether, but there were four that I knew of.

The first wedge was the one I have already mentioned—the Sunday-afternoon teas. I noticed that Dr. Rogers never talked much. Instead of talking, he listened to us, and we, I am afraid talked exclusively about ourselves. The actors who were in plays talked about their work, the actors who were not in plays talking about the opportunities waiting for them around the next corner, and the students described the illustrious futures they had planned. But Dr. Rogers, who could have found us childish and tiresome, seemed to enjoy his brief meetings with us. He always came in to tea looking tired and went out again looking less so.

When he was in the room, all of us, I think, felt a certain amount of constraint. We were quieter than we were apt to be when we had Mrs. Rogers to ourselves. But although she didn't mind how much noise we made, she wouldn't let anyone forget that this was the St. Agnes rectory, and not backstage somewhere, or a student dormitory. One time, an uncle of hers, a short, jolly man who favored black-and-white checked suits, began telling a group of us a story. Mrs. Rogers joined us, and he stopped abruptly. Putting his arm affectionately around her waist, he said, "Well, now that Alice is here, I suppose I can't go on?"

She smiled, and without sounding at all priggish, replied, "No, Jack, I'm afraid you can't."

Another of Alice Rogers' wedges was the theater. She and Dr. Rogers saw everything that was produced at the eight theatres in the parish, and a good many other productions as well, including ice shows and non-stop variety, and one January when my parents were in town for a vacation, we all went to a play together. I don't remember what it was, but I remember very well the dinner that preceded it. The Rogerses, who liked to patronize the neighborhood restaurants, suggested eating out. We all met at the Parthenon, a tiny place that had recently been opened by a Greek family named Lito. Earlier in the day, Dr. Rogers had paid a pastoral call on the Litos (he always called on the residents of the parish, whether they were Church of England or not), and they knew we were coming and turned out to welcome us. There were five of them, and they comprised the restaurant staff: Mr. and Mrs. Lito, a son, Harry, and two daughters, Elena and Marie. Marie, the younger girl, was our waitress that night. Mrs. Rogers ordered a mixed-vegetable soup that Mr. Lito recommended, and in her haste to serve it Marie slipped and poured it all into Mrs. Rogers' lap. There, on a background of rose silk, lay broccoli flowers, tomato slices, potato cubes, cabbage slivers, pearl onions, asparagus heads, strips of leek, and several varieties of bean. Marie's screams brought Elena running, and soon the whole family, other diners forgotten, stood about our table, weeping, arguing, and wringing their hands. Mrs. Rogers, her self-possession in no way impaired, quietly asked Mr. Lito and his son to fetch towels, bowls, and a mop. Then she set about comforting the hysterical women. Taking Mrs. Lito's hand in hers, she explained that her dress, though new, was made of a special material that would dry in a matter of minutes and take no stain. This was untrue. The dress was ruined.

Normally, the Rogerses went to the theatre alone; our party was an exception. Alice liked to keep up her theatrical connections. A couple of days a week, she helped at a theatre girls' residential club, and during the Christmas pantomime season she ran a club of her own for child actors in the St. Agnes crypt. Pantomimes are usually presented twice daily, and the club was open from lunchtime until after the evening show. Meals were served and games were organized, and there was a separate room fitted up with cots for artistes to take naps in.

A third wedge of relaxation that Alice evolved for her husband was their breakfast pattern. On wet days, when I went to lectures by bus instead of walking, I could see their breakfast table clearly. It was in the bay window of their bedroom, on the second floor—a large room over the living room. There they would sit, just about on a level with the tops of the passing buses, the rector in his dressing gown, eating eggs and reading the *Times,* and Alice in a pretty wrap, presiding and pouring coffee. They were assured of quiet, because their room had double windows, and they did not seem to mind the fact that otherwise they completely lacked privacy. Prudence, their bad-tempered Siamese cat, would be on the window sill nearby. It was a scene more appropriate to a country house than to a soot-covered building in central London. If I was late, Dr. Rogers would have finished breakfast. He would be smoking his pipe, sitting at the table alone, usually with his head turned a little to one side. Mrs. Tucker once told me that when I saw him that way, he was listening to Mrs. Rogers play the piano. She kept her piano farther back in the room, and she had persuaded Dr. Rogers not to make appointments before ten or ten-thirty in the morning, so that he could begin his day with a leisurely meal and a private concert. I never heard of her playing for anyone else.

But the wedge I liked best was the bells. As soon as I discovered that it was Mrs. Rogers who played the musical-comedy numbers from the St. Agnes belfry, I told her about the fine peal we had in our church at home, and how I was sometimes allowed to watch our ringers at work. I also asked how one person could handle a full set of bells by herself; bell ringing is complicated. Mrs. Rogers responded by inviting me to go with her the next time she played.

So, one morning, we met by appointment at the belfry door and climbed the spiral stone steps together. The ringers' chamber of St. Agnes church was approximately thirteen feet square and panelled in light wood, with thick coconut matting on the floor and a high ceiling pierced by a circle of eight holes for the bell ropes of the peal of eight bells. This was a familiar sight to me, and I knew that to handle the eight bells in the normal way, one man per rope would be required; bells are heavy, and one bell needs one man's attention. Each rope turns a wheel, which is attached to a bell and revolves it, swinging it against the tongue (or clapper) that hangs inside the barrel, as the casing is called. This operation takes time; there is a perceptible pause between the pull on the bell rope and the bell's reply. In addition, the sound made by the tongue hitting the inside of the barrel produces a reverberation that must also be allowed for; otherwise the whole business becomes a booming and a muddle.

I was still wondering how Mrs. Rogers was going to handle this intricate matter on her own when I noticed that near one side of the ceiling there was a row of eight smaller holes through which came a set of much smaller ropes. At a height of about six feet from the floor, these were threaded through a wooden frame, about the size of a card-table top, so that they hung straight down and only a few inches apart. These, I realized, were Mrs. Rogers' ropes, and I assumed that the purpose of the frame was to enable her to reach them all easily, but she said it was to make sure that they did not foul each other when she pulled them. "My ropes can hang in a row like that because they only control hammers on the outsides of the barrels," she told me. "It's not a method that expert ringers approve of—they think that 'clocking' a bell is apt to crack it. But it's the only way in which one person can handle a full peal. A clocked bell answers immediately, which simplifies the ringer's job, though I admit the result isn't as satisfactory to the ear. There's almost no reverberation from a clocked bell—the sound escapes at once—whereas, with the rope-and-wheel method, it's held in and escapes slowly."

While I sat on a bench against one wall, Mrs. Rogers stood before her frame with her music—big square notes like those of a child's first piano piece—set on a violin stand beside her. She concentrated, bracing the frame with her left hand and pulling the ropes sharply with her right. She played a Coward waltz that morning, and a nursery rhyme, and two of the tunes from a musical that (she told me later) she and Dr. Rogers had seen a few nights before. Then she rested a minute or two before repeating her program.

We couldn't talk while Mrs. Rogers played, but on our way down the stairs she told me a little about herself. She was a true Cockney, born within the sound of Bow bells. Her grandfather (the one who wasn't a clown) had owned an inn in Cheapside, quite close to the church of St. Mary-le-Bow. The inn had been pulled down long since and replaced by a block of offices, but during Mrs. Rogers' childhood her grandfather's home had been frequented by the Bow bell ringers, and she had sometimes persuaded them to let her watch them work. She loved bells, and she would have liked to ring with the regular St. Agnes team, but ringing changes is men's pleasure, and she had to content herself with her frame.

When Dr. Rogers heard his wife begin to play, he stopped whatever he was doing and listened until she had finished. Other people in the neighborhood did the same; the hammers on the outsides of the bells made a loud, cheerful noise one could hardly ignore. Mrs. Rogers didn't have a regular schedule for playing—special services such as weddings prevented that—but she played whenever she could, providing one more wedge for her husband, and I often watched her.

In the course of these pleasant sessions, Mrs. Rogers and I got to know each other well. I found that she enjoyed giving advice. "Always treat a proposal of marriage *seriously*," she cautioned me, as if, as was not the case, I had just received one. "That's the one time in your life when you need think only of yourself." In her opinion, students talked too much. When one time I received some flowers from a man, in a box addressed to me but with a card for another girl tucked inside, Mrs. Rogers listened to my opinion of the situation and then said, "Well, if it were me, I'd want to leave the field clear for the other girl to make a fuss. I wouldn't *say* anything. I'd just give him a big hug."

Her methods were not always successful (it saddens me that I cannot now remember whether the hug was, or even if I tried it), but her advice nearly always made sense. Once, as we emerged from the belfry stairs, we were met by a distraught young actor named Stephen, who came occasionally to the Sunday teas. Stephen had a pretty wife who had gone to New York in a play, and he was waving an eighteen-page letter from her in which she explained that she had fallen in love with someone else and wanted a divorce. He said that he must write his wife, and he didn't know what to say. Mrs. Rogers replied, "Don't write. Cable," and together they concocted a brief message ("DEAR DON'T BE SILLY"), as a result of which Stephen's wife returned, and so far as I know lived happily with him ever after.

Sometimes, going to and from the bells, I tried to get Mrs. Rogers to discuss religion, but all I ever learned about her beliefs, apart from her insistence that she wasn't a religious woman, was that, unlike most of the members of Dr. Rogers' congregations, she believed that one should shoulder one's troubles without complaining. This quickly became the core of my own faith, such as it was; I admired Mrs. Rogers very much. Changing over from the theatre to the church couldn't have been easy for her, but she never let any aspect of it get the better of her. My father reported that soon after the Rogerses were married they attended a large city banquet together. Mrs. Rogers found herself seated some distance away from her husband, and faced with an unfamiliar array of spoons, forks, knives, and glasses. Instead of worrying about which to use, she simply turned to the man sitting next to her and asked him to begin each course ahead of her so that she could follow his signals. "I don't want to embarrass my hosts by making mistakes," she said.

She was in many ways a frivolous woman, though I wouldn't then have used that word to describe her. She lived entirely in the present. She adored her husband, and she loved the theatre, playing bells, playing the piano, and making hats. In the well-ordered world she provided for Dr. Rogers, the only serious questions concerned her own millinery. As soon as she had finished making something that the rector thought looked particularly pretty on her head, she would tear it apart and remake it some other way.

I also liked hats and the theatre and bells and piano music, and since I felt so much more at home with Mrs. Rogers' interests than I did with her husband's, it puzzles me why I so often listened to his preaching. Part of the reason was custom. I found my work at the university absorbing, but weekends were apt to drag, and churchgoing was a way to pass the time—one that readily occurs to someone raised in a clerical household. I could, of course, have found some other church with a preacher who appealed to me more than Dr. Rogers did, but since on most Sundays I was already at the St. Agnes rectory for tea, it was easy to go on to church with Mrs. Rogers.

Not that I found the services dull. We sang popular hymns, and the preacher, with his steel-gray hair, dark eyes, and tremendous sincerity, was spellbinding. At the beginning of the sermon, all the lights in the church would be turned out except for one spot above Dr. Rogers' head, and his congregations would sit breathless. I was swept along by him as much as anyone else, and it was only afterward, when I thought about what he had said, that he didn't seem to make sense to me. He always talked about the same things—about hope and encouragement and consolation, and he addressed his remarks without exception to the middle-aged and elderly who thronged his church. I felt that these people, with their college examinations behind them and their careers and marriage partners long ago settled, were far less in need of encouragement than those of us who still had these vital decisions to make. One day, I said as much to Mrs. Rogers, and she laughed. I tried to get her to admit that she agreed, but she only said, "It's no good trying to make me talk about religion—I won't. Sometimes Lewis wants to, but if he once begins bringing work home, when's he going to get any rest?"

I told her that in my home there were no such restrictions. On Sunday mornings, I always listened with the closest attention to my father's sermons in the hope that I should be able to catch him out (in a misattributed quotation, for example) and bring my catch to luncheon. But I didn't enlarge on the subject to Mrs. Rogers. She had a polite but firm way of heading off a conversation if she didn't want to pursue it.

She could be quite firm when she wished. Usually I approved of her behavior and liked to emulate it, but there was one occasion when I didn't approve at all, and that was the Christmas when she persuaded me and a number of the other students who went regularly to her Sunday teas to take part in a pageant she directed. I had appeared in church pageants before, and I had enjoyed dressing up and strutting about. But Mrs. Rogers brought an unwelcome professional touch to the proceedings. She insisted on endless rehearsals and no strutting. ("I don't feel reverent when I'm floodlit," I complained at one point. "You're not here to feel reverent," Mrs. Rogers retorted. "You're here to keep awake and watch your cues.")

A full week of performances was given in St. Agnes sanctuary, with professional singers augmenting the regular choir and a professional orchestra helping out the organist. Two young artists, who later made names for themselves as dress designers, were brought in to do our clothes. Mrs. Rogers gave Dr. Rogers the only speaking part—that of narrator of the Christmas story—and all that the rest of us were permitted to do was to move at intervals from chalk mark to chalk mark on the floors of the nave and chancel. The pageant was a tremendous success, and Mrs. Rogers was eager to do it again the following year, but we remembered how demanding she had been, and how disapproving when we overstepped our chalk. No one would volunteer for a second production, and the project had to be abandoned.

My father was amused when I told him how disagreeable I had found the pageant. I wanted him to know that I still thought highly of Mrs. Rogers in spite of it, so I added an account of her belief in cheerfulness at all costs and her dislike of complaint and whining. My father wasn't as impressed as I had supposed he would be. He said, "That's all right as far as it goes, and in an emergency it could be all a man needs."

I was disappointed with this remark. I didn't follow what he meant, and I couldn't persuade him to expand on it.

The June I graduated, Dr. Rogers died. He collapsed without warning during Evensong, and died of a brain hemorrhage an hour or two later. I had already gone home for the summer. I heard it announced over the radio. There was a special broadcast program the next day, with excerpts from some of Dr. Rogers' sermons, and there were long obituaries in the newspapers. The funeral service at St. Agnes was conducted by the Bishop of London. Through all the strain and the publicity, Mrs. Rogers behaved exactly as I had known she would—cheerfully, and without any whining. There were pictures of her in the Sunday press shaking hands with people and smiling.

My parents wrote to her, and so did I—a stilted little note that didn't say any of the things I wanted it to say. Mrs. Rogers replied individually to each of us. In my letter, she said that she would soon be moving out of the St. Agnes rectory, taking Prudence and Noah with her, though not Mrs. Tucker. She wouldn't be going far. She'd been offered an apartment on the top floor of the theatre girls' club, and one of the attractions of her new home was that there was plenty of room for tea parties. She intended to go on having them on Sundays as before, and she hoped I would come often.

I fully intended to go. I also intended to write to Mrs. Rogers again and ask her to go on playing the bells. I knew that of course this would depend on whether or not the new rector wanted her to play them, but I assumed he wouldn't change established customs right away. But my letter never got written, and if there were other people who meant to ask Mrs. Rogers the same thing, they must have forgotten to write, too. After Dr. Rogers died, there was no more Noel Coward music on the St. Agnes bells.

Dr. Rogers' successor wasn't appointed for several months. He turned out to be a young man with a young family and a reputation as a youth leader. I don't know how successful he was. By the end of that summer, I had started my first job, and given up being young myself.

Although I had meant to drop in on Mrs. Rogers for tea, for one reason or another the weeks went by and I spent my Sundays doing other things. I only saw her once again. We met quite by chance one morning in a crowded London street: it must have been a year or more after Dr. Rogers' death. Mrs. Rogers didn't see me, she was oblivious of everyone, I think, and I was startled because instead of the serene and pleasant expression I was accustomed to see on her face, she looked angry.

Suddenly, I understood my father's remark about cheerfulness and not whining being all that a person might need in an emergency. Mrs. Rogers' emergency was over, and I knew, just as clearly as if she had told me, that what she was angry about was her widowhood. Whatever tools she needed to cope with the present situation she hadn't got, and if Dr. Rogers in his lifetime had had them, he hadn't been allowed to bring them home. I didn't make myself known to Alice that morning out of fright. I was alarmed to discover that faith—whatever the faith—doesn't drop in one's path like an apple off a tree. It has to be worked for, attended to, watched over, and grown, the way a garden must, or a friendship. Or love.

Michael

The present-day Mrs. Rogers, the one in the bed next to mine, was a loud, merry lady with a great many loud, merry friends. The friends came in schools to visit her, six or eight at a time, and occasionally the Floor Nurse would shoo the outer reaches of them into the corridor, where they would await their turn, cackling and flapping and disturbing everyone. So far as I can recall, Mrs. Rogers only had one visitor who came by himself to see her and was quiet about it—he was a distant cousin, she told me later—a tall drainpipe of a man with a shock of blond hair, large gentle blue eyes and a badly-scarred hare lip.

It was the hare lip that set me journeying into the recesses of my memory again. When I saw Mrs. Rogers's visitor, I knew that he, like the young man lurking in my memory, had probably spent the first eighteen years of his life in and out of hospitals. That had been the lot of Michael Rawlinson, whose father was a General Practitioner in the small town near the New Forest (I'll call it Pinewood) in which an aunt of mine lived. Michael had been born with a very badly cleft palate.

The Rawlinson family—there were two older children, both girls—treated Michael with great good sense: they never permitted him to feel sorry for himself. Although they couldn't prevent him from realizing that his childhood and youth were different from other boys', they impressed upon him that what a man does not have can be almost as much of a talent for living as what he has. One of Michael's problems was his lack of a normal education. The gaps in his schooling caused by his long and frequent hospital stays meant that he grew up almost illiterate. The Rawlinsons arranged tutoring for him, but it didn't work out too well. The strain of the operations sapped Michael's energy so that even during the periods when he was home and supposedly in reasonably good health, he didn't feel like doing much except sit about.

Despite his semi-invalidism, Michael never seemed to envy the people who were born with better-looking faces than his. It was as if, in a world populated by tightrope-walkers, he was perfectly happy to be down below, holding the net. He made friends easily, particularly among people older than he. Betty Parker, his favorite friend when he was 18, was 25. Betty was Dr. Rawlinson's nurse-receptionist, and to say that Michael was in love with her would be to give his feelings far too definite a label: he would have shied off in alarm if anyone had suggested such a thing. But the summer he was 18 he did think about Betty a good deal, and he would find himself making excuses to drop by his father's office on Pinewood's main street when he had no real reason to go there.

Since that was the extent of the relationship—smiling and saying hello across a reception desk—it wasn't surprising that Michael was able to accept without heartbreak the news that Betty was to be married. He was invited to the wedding, and he would certainly have gone—Betty's home was only in the next town—but he was undergoing the last of his operations at the time. The man Betty married—his name was Arthur Benning—was American (but a very decent chap, Dr. Rawlinson reported.) Betty found time to write to Michael in hospital and send him a piece of her wedding cake. In her letter, she invited him to come and visit in Massachusetts. Michael looked up Massachusetts in his father's one-volume atlas as soon as he had the chance. He was disappointed, though the place would, he supposed, seem less cramped once one got there.

When Michael was twenty, he set himself up in business. His line was lawn-care. Pinewood's quite large community of retired people—including my aunt—were fond of gardening, but considerably less fond of following a lawn-mower, and Michael's services were soon in demand. His knowledge of grass-growing, picked up from his father, was sound. The Rawlinsons had a beautiful lawn on which the doctor lavished all his spare time. In two years, Michael went from a one-man, one-machine operation to one man, two boys, and a small pick-up truck that would carry three mowers. In addition, he was prepared, if asked, to handle other duties. He would walk dogs and water houseplants, and if a client were sick, cook a meal and wash dishes. I remember one September when I was spending a few days in Pinewood hearing my aunt say: "Thank you very much, Michael. I do so dislike it when the time comes to light the furnace! Right away it starts driving out all the nice dampness we've been building up all summer . . ."

Michael was twenty-five when he decided to take a vacation. Leaving the boys to handle the business under Dr. Rawlinson's supervision, he bought a $99 bus ticket—a kind of ticket that was only available to visitors from overseas—and set off to spend six weeks touring the U.S.A. New York was to be his base—his elder sister was now married to a Swiss and living in Brooklyn—and in addition to all the places mentioned in the bus brochure, he planned to visit Betty and Arthur. Every year, the invitation had been repeated on the Benning's Christmas Card.

The trip worked out extraordinarily well. Among the places Michael saw were the Grand Canyon, Yellowstone, the Rockies, San Francisco, Yosemite, and New Orleans. He liked the people he met and the food he ate and he did his best not to appear as appalled as he was at the damage excessive sunshine and clear skies can do to lawns. In order to

save time and money, he sightsaw by day and slept on his bus by night—
one of the things he had learned from his hospital experiences was how
to sleep well at any time, anywhere. His last stop before flying home
was to be with the Bennings, at a beach cottage they owned on a Massachusetts lake. He had written to Betty in plenty of time, and she had
replied inviting him for her birthday. She enclosed a map, and told him
where to tell the bus driver to drop him off.

The Benning visit was the only part of Michael's tour that went agley.
In Memphis, Tennessee, his bus company came out on strike. When he
made enquiries, a harassed official advised him to take the next available plane or train north if he wished to make sure of his connections
to England.

The notion of coming all this way without even setting eyes on Betty
at all was more than Michael could bear. Nevertheless, he bought a
stamped postcard and sent it off telling the Bennings not to expect him,
though he would continue to do his best to see them, he said. After he
had mailed the card, it occurred to Michael that although he had never
in his life set out on a journey without first making reservations—his
$99 bus ticket was supposed always to provide a place where he could
at least sit down—this was America, and he would do as he understood
Americans did when they wanted to get somewhere: he would hitch-
hike. Thus emboldened, Michael stepped out into the street beside the
bus station, and in next to no time he was on his way.

Seven private cars and one truck later (the truck was full of bread
being driven from the central bakery of a restaurant chain) Michael
found himself at a crossroads in Otis, Massachusetts, six miles from
Betty's cottage. The date was the day after Betty's birthday, and the
time four o'clock in the morning.

Carrying his suitcase and burberry, Michael walked the six miles, but
he didn't mind—he could hardly knock on Betty's door before seven.
He found his way easily. The road, hard-surfaced except for the last

mile and a half, climbed steeply through woods of pine and maple. The last part, which was gravel, ran along behind half a dozen cottages that faced the lake. The last one, at the end of the road, had the name Benning on the mailbox.

Betty's cottage appeared to be bigger and more solidly built than the others—a house, really. It was made of pink painted wood and it had a slate roof. It was all on one floor at road level, but the ground fell away sharply beside the house so that a boat could be run in underneath. Between the house and the lake there was a lawn with a circular flower-bed surrounding a rock. A large white car—an American car, of course—was parked across the road from the front door.

Michael put his coat and suitcase down and made for the lawn. It looked to be in excellent shape, and a poke with his pocket-knife confirmed this, although he would recommend some rolling. Stepping carefully over the flower-bed, he climbed up the rock and sat down where he had a view of the water. It was a fine lake about half a mile wide, and it stretched a couple of miles or more, he judged, to his left and right. Across from him, grayish-green wooded hills folded into one another, reminding him of Windermere in the English lakes, where he had once spent a holiday after a particularly lengthy operation. Silvery mist wafted over the nearby shallows, and the silence was such that when he climbed back down from the rock and picked one of Betty's flowers—a bunchy-headed double petunia—the snap of the stalk sounded as sharp as a popgun.

At seven o'clock on the nose Michael made his way to the front of the house. He was about to ring the bell when he noticed that the door was ajar. Without quite realizing what he was doing, he gave it a push and walked in.

He found himself (immediately) in the Benning's living-room. The shades were drawn, but enough light was coming through them to reveal the shambles the place was in. On every piece of furniture, including a number of small folding tables that were dotted about, were dirty glasses, used plates, cups, saucers, knives and silver, bottles (mostly empty), and loaded ashtrays. There were serving dishes with the remains of food—congealed meat, pieces of chicken, bread, celery, tomato, pickles, fruit pie. A cup half full of black coffee had shreds of tobacco floating in it. On the floor as well as the tables were colored paper balls, which on closer inspection turned out to be used paper-napkins. In among the debris, but off the floor, were boxes of candy with wrappings and ribbons beside them. There were a dozen or more birthday cards lying about, and a bright yellow stuffed bear.

An open door to Michael's right led into the kitchen. Again, quite without realizing what he was doing, he walked over there, picking up, from force of habit because it was what he would have done at home, a couple of dirty plates and three tumblers and taking them with him.

The kitchen was in even worse confusion than the living-room. Michael had to make space on the shelf beside the sink before he could set the plates and glasses down. He was about to go back to the front door and ring the bell when it occurred to him that the Bennings must need their sleep after this much of a party, and he should wait for them to wake of their own accord. He stood about for a while doing nothing except keep quiet, and then the mess and muddle got the better of him and he began straightening up the kitchen and stacking together the stuff that had to be washed. He kept expecting that the noise he was making would disturb the Bennings, but when it didn't and he had the kitchen more or less in order, there seemed no reason why he should stop, so he went to work on the living-room.

By eight he had cleared away the dishes, emptied the ashtrays, put the paper-napkins and the present-wrappings in a waste-basket, and placed the folding tables in a rack he found for them behind the kitchen door. At eight-fifteen he ran a sinkful of hot water. The water gushed in with a roar, but there was no sound from the rear of the house, and

Michael started in on the glasses, plates, cups, saucers, knives, and silver. There were soaps and scrubbers beside the sink and when the towels hanging over the sink-shelf were too wet to do any more good, he found some more in a drawer. It was nine by the time everything was washed, dried, and neatly stacked.

Suddenly it occurred to Michael that the white car might not belong to the Bennings after all. They might have changed their plans and be away from home, and if they were, he had cleaned up after a party of burglars. Worse, Betty and her husband might have been murdered. In a panic, he ran through to the rear of the house, and suddenly, straight ahead of him through another open door, he saw Betty.

She was asleep, lying on her side in a big double bed, facing him and naked. She had thrown back the covers below her waist, and one breast leaned heavily on the other, the nipples dark against her light, glowing skin. Her hair clung close to her small head, and her lashes were spread on her cheeks as if drawn there with an etching pen. She breathed evenly, and smiled as she breathed: a remote, utterly happy woman.

Beyond her, a shapeless lump on the far side of the bed indicated the presence of Arthur. Arthur lay with his back to his wife, muffled to the ears in blankets and motionless as a stone. Nothing of him showed except some auburn tufts sunk deep in a thick pillow.

The sight of Arthur jolted Michael into realizing what he was doing—trespassing, breaking-in, really, on the privacy of a woman he hadn't seen for years and a man he had never met. Michael didn't care a fig about Arthur, but what would Betty think if she woke and found him standing over her, staring? He turned and ran.

He covered the ground back to the Otis crossroads fast. His hitchhiking luck held. By evening, he was in Brooklyn.

Michael intended to write Betty a letter when he got back to England, telling her about finding her house and sitting on the rock and perhaps even admitting to the cleaning up. He would have liked to describe his visit amusingly and entertainingly, and add how glad he was that she could be so happy with her stranger, three-thousand miles from home. He would of course never be able to tell her what the visit had really meant to him—of how, for a moment, he had shared in her happiness and seen her as he didn't know other human beings could be seen: as strong and complete and vulnerable and touched with glory.

Michael tried to write a couple of times, but he didn't manage anything that satisfied him. Then he thought he might add a note to his next Christmas Card, but he didn't manage that, either. The card he selected—a picture of Nelson's flagship in full sail—was sold to him by one of his lawn customers, in aid of a mission to seamen. It was a nice big card, but the message-space inside had already been appropriated by a printed appeal concerning overseas milk-bars for sailors.

A Special Occasion

The only items of feminine beauty that I seriously covet are handsome eyes. If a fairy godmother had given me a choice of blessings prior to my birth, that is what I would have asked for—large, beautiful eyes in (preferably) a deep violet shade. Violet eyes was what I noticed first about Mrs. Rogers's successor in the other bed. They belonged to a fifteen-year-old belle named Linda Haight. Linda had been rushed to hospital one Sunday afternoon, suffering from stomach pains. These eased off in a few hours, but the authorities kept her where she was for several days to conduct tests. Linda, I soon learned, was the eldest of four, and so far as I could tell, she was the kingpin that kept her home together. Both her parents worked full time, and apart from driving her to the hospital that Sunday afternoon and picking her up again a week later, they paid singularly little attention to her needs. Linda didn't appear to mind, though. What she lacked in parental affection she made up in the love of her peers. The telephone never stopped ringing, and neither did the flow of teenage visitors. Linda's circle were great gossips and great repeaters of gossip. What A said to B was reported to Linda not only by A and B themselves, but also by C and D, who had had it second-hand and wanted to be in on the act. It was only at night, therefore, that Linda had to resort to communicating with me. We dined—if that is the right word for our bowls of chicken broth and crackers—at five o'clock, and although visitors were allowed until (I think) eight, mine preferred to come by daylight, and Linda's had their homework to do. We therefore filled in the long hours of the night (neither of us could sleep very well) by me telling Linda, slowly, because of my scribbling pad, a kind of movie-serial story. It was about the only other girl I had known who had large violet eyes. Her name was Yolande Cookham, and in addition to her marvelous eyes, she was slender and small and beautifully proportioned, with a pale oval face and shining black hair.

Yolande had been a college friend of mine, and we renewed acquaintance in 1943, when I ran into her quite by chance in the entrance hall of the British wartime ministry where I was then working. I was enormously pleased to see her again because my mind at that moment of meeting was full of an unattractive subject. I had just won a battle with a retired General of the Army who headed the largest of the ministry's divisions, as a result of which the General's most expert linguist (according to the General) had been fired. The linguist—I will call him Roger Curwell—spoke eight languages, and his work, accurate and fast, was respected by everybody. Unfortunately, he coupled this attribute with another. He was a Peeping Tom.

I had achieved what I wanted, which was Curwell's departure. Nevertheless, now that the fight was over, I felt uncomfortable about it. Curwell wasn't young, and even in wartime it wasn't easy for a man in his fifties to find a job. In the mood I was in, nothing could have been better medicine for me than Yolande. Yolande never felt upset about anything, least of all her own actions. Once something was done, she put it behind her and forgot about it, and she would, I knew, advise me to do the same when I told her about Roger Curwell. She and I hadn't met for a couple of years, not since we both lived in the same students' residence in London, but we thought of ourselves as friends. Yolande was a rootless, independent girl, difficult to keep in touch with once she had left the residence because she moved frequently without leaving a forwarding address. Her charm for me lay in her liveliness and energy: she seemed to squeeze twice as much entertainment out of everyday living as the rest of us. She looked enchanting that morning, I thought. She had always known how to make the best of herself, and while I, in damp, dowdy London, was suitably dressed in long-wearing tweeds and stout shoes, Yolande had on a bright, multi-colored skirt with a matching jacket, and thin slippers.

We hugged each other, and Yolande, crinkling her nose, said she might have known she would find me up to my eyes in war work in the dullest Government Department yet devised. She added that she had a hundred things to tell me, but she was on an errand; she couldn't stop to talk. Would I meet her for lunch? She named a French place a block up the street. I said I would love to, and we hugged again.

Yolande was right about my being up to my eyes in war work, but wrong in her estimation that the ministry was dull. Although our main job—censorship—was fairly routine, we also handled the release of news, and a host of activities aimed at fostering civilian morale. The staff ranged from established Civil Servants, transferred from older ministries to keep the rest of us in line, to recruits from publishing and the arts. We had a number of language experts, and a big block of female conscripts—women between the ages of 19 and 51 were subject to the draft in the same way that men were.

As a Government Department that existed only in wartime, we had no building of our own. We were housed in a commandeered college of London University. The place wasn't adequate for our needs (plywood partitions were put up in the lecture-theatres and study halls, on the ostrich principle that if you can't see the man who is working a few feet away from you, you can't hear him, either) but it had one notable advantage. There were two well-ventilated, reasonably bomb-proof floors

below ground. The upper one contained a cafeteria and a series of pho-
tographic dark rooms, the lower had a large walk-in closet lined with
shelves, and a First-Aid Room. Almost all the rest of the space, except
for corridors and restrooms, was filled with furniture and filing cabinets
belonging to the College.

Most of the ministry's divisions worked around the clock, and because train and bus services were apt to be dislocated by air-raids, sleeping accommodation was provided at the building for anyone who
wanted it. Rows of doubledecker bunks were put along the corridors of
both below-ground floors: the men were given the upper floor and the
women the lower. The closet on the women's floor was turned into an
office at which one registered for a bunk and drew a bedding-bundle—
two Government-issue blankets and one Government-issue pillow.

Sleeping at the ministry was not comfortable, though it was better
than travelling home late and alone in the blackout. Shift-hours varied
among the different divisions, and there was a great deal of coming and
going all night. Some of the staff made no attempt to sleep. Others
didn't reserve bunks in advance but came down in the small hours and
prowled about among the sleepers looking for a vacant perch. The clerk
in charge of bedding locked up at nine, but before he left he stacked
any blanket bundles he had left over in the hall outside his office, which
was across from the stairs and elevators on our floor. The arrangement
was rather haphazard, but it seemed to work.

I always tried to find a bunk as far away from the bedding store as I
could because the first of the screened-off sleeping areas, the one nearest the store, had been adopted by our teletypists. These girls—there
were usually half a dozen of them on duty at a time—ran a kind of
permanent party in that section of corridor, gossiping, singing, occasionally fighting, squealing with laughter, and comparing notes at the
tops of their voices on clothes, make-up, hair-styles, and dates.

The rest of us could have slept better if the teletypists had reserved their hilarity for the daytime, or at least turned their lights out, but we all had our own ways of coping with the London blitz, and this was theirs. They were an empty-headed, merry, highly sociable group who in peacetime earned a living as film extras, models, pantomime chorus dancers, movie-house ushers, and, when driven to it, waitresses in what were often family-owned cafes and bars. For most of them (they were all conscripts) the ministry was the first employer they had ever had who offered them not only a training but also the assurance, at least while the war lasted, of a steady job. This in itself raised problems. Regular employment, if you are not accustomed to it, can be very fatiguing, and the girls' pay was appallingly low. Miss Marsh, their supervisor, a stout woman in her thirties, took the practical view that the girls had to supplement their Government incomes somehow if they were to manage. "I know what the talk is," she told me, "I've got ears, but they don't any of them go on the streets. Why should they, when there's all these nice Service Clubs? Girls need their fun the same as boys, and boys can afford to pay for it. But same as the boys, they'd die for Mr. Churchill any time."

Dying for Mr. Churchill was something we all faced fairly often. Whenever we emerged from a night below ground, we had no idea whether the homes we had left the day before would still be standing when we got back to them.

A day after day situation of this sort makes one edgy. Under peacetime conditions, Roger Curwell's peeping need never have cost him his job. The girls would have made a joke of the episode and dealt summarily with it themselves—thought of some way of making a fool of him that would have kept him out of their hair. But this was not peacetime, and the Curwell affair made a splendid hook on which to hang their frustration over living, or trying to live, in a city under siege.

What happened was that one evening quite late, Roger Curwell found himself alone on our floor. He picked up the last bundle of blankets that had been left out, and as he walked away he noticed a crack in the screen that separated the hallway from the teletypists' party. The usual merrymaking was going on, and Curwell tiptoed over and had a peep at it. The next night that he was on duty, he came back for more.

The girls probably didn't catch him at his peeping for several nights, but when they did the sound of their fury filled the entire basement. It was unfortunate for Curwell that so many small factors combined to work against him. If he had not had to take his turn at the night shift, or if the bedding store had not been on our floor, or if the teletypists had slept during their sleeping time instead of parading up and down their corridor squawking and preening themselves in their underwear, the problem might never have arisen. As it was, however, the girls chose to do the one thing guaranteed to turn a small, if awkward, episode into a Case. They made a formal protest in writing.

Somebody who didn't like Roger Curwell had helped them: the protest was worded in correct Civil Service-ese and set out as it was supposed to be, in quadruplicate. It arrived on my desk one September afternoon. Pinned to it was a note from my boss, the chief personnel officer, saying that since a moral issue appeared to be involved it was for me to look into; my father was a Church of England clergyman, whereas his merely bred racehorses.

I knew Roger Curwell well enough by sight. He was a tall, strikingly handsome man with slightly stooping shoulders and pepper and salt gray hair. He had an ingratiating, very charming smile and a quiet manner. He looked as if, in peacetime life, he might have been a schoolmaster. The information in his personal file was sparse. He was 53, the son of an Army officer, and he had held a great many jobs with business firms in different parts of the world, working as an interpreter or translator. He had been divorced and had remarried shortly before the outbreak of war.

An official complaint meant a lot of work. Everything connected with it, every telephone call and discussion, had to be confirmed in writing and placed on file. My job was to assemble all the relevant information and present it with a resume to the personnel officer for his decision.

I began with Miss Marsh. Her attitude, normally easy and relaxed, was, in the matter of Curwell's peeping, fiercely partisan. She said that the girls had been insulted, that no Peeping Tom ever changed his ways, and that Curwell must be fired immediately.

The ministry was short of good linguists, and I knew we must keep Curwell if we could. I said that the personnel department and the censorship division would look into alternative possibilities for him (that was a fine Civil Service phrase, 'looking into alternative possibilities') and that the girls could rest assured he wouldn't give them any more trouble. I added that I knew the General would be as distressed as the rest of us were over what had happened.

I was wrong. The General, an unpleasant little man, took the view that the whole thing was a put-up job. He said that Curwell's behavior had always been exemplary and his work excellent, and that he had problems of his own: Curwell's wife, it seemed, was very sick. It was clear to me that the General resented having to discuss staff matters with so junior a member of the personnel department as myself instead of with the racehorse-breeder's son, but he did agree to tell Curwell that a complaint about him had been made.

I hoped (naïvely) that this was all that would be required, but within a couple of days Curwell peeped again, and this time I saw him myself.

It was two o'clock in the morning, and I had just come off firewatch duty on the ministry roof—a job that everybody in personnel had to take his turn at. I went below to go to bed, and as I passed the end of the teletypists' corridor (it was comparatively quiet there that night— just a radio playing loudly, and all the lights on) I saw Curwell bending over with his eye to the screen. The crack in it had been repaired, but the material was only thin board, and he had either made, or found, another place to look through.

I had a semi-side view, but I was astonished at how Curwell's peeping changed him. He looked diminished and shrivelled: a shut-out alley-cat of a man. I said his name, and he jumped round—at a loss, but only for a moment. Then he muttered some remark that I didn't catch, smiled, and slipped past me up the stairs.

I went to sleep intending to report on Curwell first thing in the morning, but during the night, the apartment I was then sharing with a friend was bombed. Fortunately neither of us was home at the time and there were no casualties, but the building, a converted mews, was completely destroyed. I spent most of the next two days filling out claim forms (the Government had insured everybody against enemy damage) and sorting through the rubble in the hope of finding some of our possessions. When I finally returned to work, I wrote my report on Curwell, and in order to save time I carried it over to the General.

It was a mistake, I suppose, to assume that I would be treated any more civilly this time than last. What I asked was to have Curwell put permanently on day shifts, an arrangement that would retain his services but remove his opportunity to antagonize and embarrass the girls. The General replied that when he needed advice on how to run his division he was glad to know where he could come for it. I seemed to have forgotten, he said, that there was a war on, and that if the censorship division was to operate efficiently, special arrangements could not be made to suit the convenience of an individual member of the staff. And then he added, with a creaky little smile, that my concern for the girls' reputations struck him as unrealistic in view of common ministry knowledge. It was not as if Curwell had been caught peeping at any of the *ladies* on the staff. The teletypists, if I would pardon him for speaking frankly, were nothing but a bunch of Soho tarts.

I thought at first that I hadn't heard ar: ght. When I realized that I had, I opened my mouth to reply, but suddenly some other person seemed to take me over and speak on my behalf. This person spoke about the teletypists, but in her remarks she included all my feelings about the war—my accummulated terror, horror, confusion, disgust, and anger. She did not boil over with these feelings, however. She released them singly, in slivers of ice, using a language of understatement for which an English accent is extraordinarily well suited. I had not known that I had so much nastiness in me, and I was impressed.

I told the General—or, more accurately, I listened to my voice telling the General—that since he had reminded me that there was a war on, perhaps the time had come for me to remind him why. We were not, I said, fighting to keep the ministry staffed with expert linguists, nor even to preserve the security of the nation by means of a competently-run censorship division. We were fighting to ensure that teletypists—those alive now and those who would take their places in the future—would be treated with decency and grace. What a girl chose to do with her time when she was outside the ministry, my voice continued, was her own affair, but once within the building, the Government regarded *all* women members of the staff as ladies.

I made a pompous exhibition of myself, but the General didn't seem to think so: he paid me the compliment of looking quite alarmed. When I had finished, I didn't wait for him to speak. I hurried back to my office, where I wrote up our conversation while it was still, as it were, freezing on my lips. Then I marked the file to the chief personnel officer with a note saying that the matter was now for his decision.

But as it turned out, it was for mine.

The Director-General of the ministry was a peacetime barrister whom I will call Lord Colwyn. His job, so far as I understood it, was to see that the different wheels of our organization meshed more or less as they were supposed to do, and that objectives involving the news media, advertizing, films, and the arts were achieved without contravening too many Treasury Regulations. Lord Colwyn was a tall man with thick, curly black hair, a beaked nose, and large, heavy-lidded eyes. When one met him shuffling through the corridors of the ministry he appeared to be half asleep: a deceptive impression. Behind the dormant, parrot face was an agile mind with a strong grasp of its surroundings. Lord Colwyn had a comfortable office on the second floor, but he didn't use it much. He preferred to sit on an old sofa in the corridor outside, where he could catch people easily as they went by, and chat with them without the formality of an appointment.

One of Lord Colwyn's methods of working was to pounce on operational files as they travelled about the building in the messenger service. This service was operated by a flock of elderly clerks—the two on our floor were known as Ninety-Nine and A-Hundred—who picked up files at strategic points and carried them to a central registry, from which, after a delay of several hours, they were collected again, and redistributed. It was against the rules for files to be moved without the intervention of the messenger service, but of course we all did such moving from time to time, and the worst offender was the Director-General. Passing a tray of files at a collection point, Lord Colwyn would scoop up half a dozen and bear them off to his sofa, where he would select a couple for study and opinion. The opinion would usually consist of half a dozen words, added in black ink with a very broad pen.

Thus it was that an hour after I started the Curwell file on its journey to the chief personnel officer, it arrived back on my desk. Across the last memorandum, Lord Colwyn had written: "I support Miss Warren's decision."

This was fine. It meant that although I hadn't reached a decision—up to that moment, I hadn't been entitled to one—when I did, it would stick.

I suppose it quite often happens that a man loses his job because another man ought to. Curwell's peeping seemed to me much less of a menace than the General's attitude, but Curwell was within my grasp, and the General was not.

"Well, quite a little experience, wasn't it?" Miss Marsh said brightly when I told her that Curwell was on his way out.

"That's one way of looking at it," I said.

"Oh, I didn't mean *him,*" she continued. "The ones with the style to them are always the worst, and I've said all along that the sooner somebody popped him down a drain the better. None of the chaps in Censorship liked him, you know. I expect you guessed it was them that wrote our complaint for us—put the proper language in. No, I mean the way things get done here—like us being believed. That was *nice . . .*"

It hadn't felt like a little experience to me, which was why it seemed so good to be meeting Yolande for lunch. I knew she would be amused to hear about my battle for the teletypists, and that she would laugh at my crusading and restore my sense of proportion.

When Yolande and I had first met at the student residence, I was in my second year at King's College, and she had just started at the Slade School of Art. Of the twenty young women who roomed on the third floor of the residence, Yolande, at seventeen, was the youngest, though she seemed much older. Most of us were on our own for the first time in our lives, but Yolande had been living independently for years. Her parents were divorced—her father lived in Yorkshire and her mother in Paris. That background would have been enough to single Yolande out from the rest of us, but what distinguished her in our eyes—gave her style, *cachet,* and an envied sophistication, was that she had a part-time job and a lover.

The job was in her father's London office—Mr. Cookham was in the wool trade and he usually spent two days of each week in town. Her job consisted mostly of running errands and taking buyers to lunch, but it brought in what seemed to me a princely salary. In spite of this Yolande was usually in financial straits and borrowing money from the rest of us . Her life-style was a mixture of extravagance (taxis and out-of-season flowers) and cheese-paring (she knew how to travel all over London on a single penny Underground ticket. At certain stations, the ticket-collector's barrier could be avoided by running up five flights of emergency stairs.)

Yolande was an expensive girl to know, but she was also lively and affectionate and, for some of us, an education. Crinkling her nose, she would make fun of our devotion to sports ("You are off to field hockey again, I see by your tool,") giggle over the institutional meals we uncomplainingly ate (the residence catering was strong on cabbage, brussels sprouts, boiled potatoes, and prunes), and comment on our clothes. ("Now that's what I call a really *sensible* dress! Nothing that wasn't utterly sensible could ever happen to you in that dress . . .") Her own wardrobe was elegant and anything but sensible. While the rest of us took to raincoats, umbrellas, and rubbers when it rained, Yolande tripped about wet as a water rat, her thin shoes squelching as she walked.

Her criticism might be teasing, but it was always kind, and because of that it gave us pause: we began to see ourselves as the overgrown schoolgirls that most of us were. In return, we tried to provide Yolande with more than emergency cash. We tried to give her some of the mothering that her background lacked. She had grown up in hotels all over Europe, and although that had taught her how to take care of herself, it hadn't supplied her with roots. We subjected her to something of the same kind of treatment we had been subjected to in our own homes, and she responded in much the way we had—with amusement, exasperation, and love. We ironed and mended her clothes, we made her start her day with a respectable breakfast, we bought her waterproof boots to wear over her ridiculous shoes, and when she needed a dentist we found her one, and went with her to the appointment. We told each other that we would have done the same for anyone in Yolande's situation, but this was not true. We cared for Yolande the way we did because she had the lover.

Men did not bulk large in our lives. In fact it cannot be said that they bulked at all. We dated the male students occasionally, but not with much enthusiasm. Most of us assumed, I think, that we would marry one day, but this would be after we were through with lectures, seminars, term papers, and examinations. Yolande's schedule—Art School, part-time job, a weekend man—struck me as ambitious but exhausting. Not that any of the men I knew had suggested becoming my lover, not even when I rented the Twopenny Room.

The Twopenny Room was a small room in the basement of the residence that could be hired for private entertaining. It cost two pence an hour, or fourpence if the makings of a coal fire were included. The room contained a sofa, two chairs, a coffee table, a bright overhead light and a hooked rug, and the walls were hung with jolly hunting prints. I didn't find it a particularly romantic setting, but then I never really gave the place its head. The only times I rented the Twopenny Room I went the full fourpenny splash, but my beau and I spent the whole hour trying to get the fire going.

Yolande rather disturbed us by saying that unless we took lovers we would turn out as barren as twigs. When I reported this to my parents, my father said he didn't think I should attach too much weight to Yolande's understanding of biology, but that I should watch my finances where she was concerned, and *give* her what money I thought I could afford, rather than lend it. My mother merely observed that there had been a Cookham at Cheltenham Ladies College when she was there— a homely girl who would have been lying if she had said she had a lover.

But Yolande was not lying. We knew from the effect that Peter had on her (Peter was as much of her man's name as she would divulge) that she wasn't making him up. He came to London almost every Saturday, and the moment he telephoned, Yolande would drop everything and rush off to meet him at some airport, railroad station, or hotel. When she came back—late Sunday night or early Monday morning—she would seem recharged and glowing. One felt one could warm one's hands at her face.

Yolande never said much about Peter. In time, I learned that he travelled for an export-import firm, and that in his background were a wife and two sons. I was curious to meet him. I kept trying to imagine what kind of man could inspire such selfless devotion in a girl not too much given to selflessness about anything. Yolande said she would try to arrange a meeting, but that it couldn't be at the residence: Peter didn't care about women in a crowd.

When I asked if he intended to divorce his wife and marry her, Yolande said I was *bourgeoise*. She told me that the kind of relationship they had didn't have intentions—it was already perfect the way it was. And certainly she behaved as if this were true. She seemed to all of us enviably and ecstatically happy.

The residence authorities believed that Yolande went home to her father at the weekends, and when the truth got out, as eventually it did, she was asked to leave. We helped her find a furnished room, and we made new curtains and slipcovers for it because Yolande thought the ones already there were ugly. We promised to see her often, but the new place was across Hyde Park from the residence, and meetings were hard to arrange. Then her telephone was cut off because she hadn't paid the bill, and after that she moved and failed to tell us where she had gone.

I missed Yolande very much. Without her, I had better nights ("Are you awake? I've got this taxi waiting. Did you know they're allowed to charge more if it's after three?") But I also had duller days. Mr. Cookham's London office was not used solely for wool-trade business. A Cookham uncle operated a Turf Consultant's there. This was perfectly legal, but from remarks that Yolande let fall, I gathered that the family indulged in a variety of bookmaking enterprises that were not always within the law, and which helped explain why she was usually hard up. Yolande flattered me by assuming that I would know all about the fun of placing after-hours bets and dodging the authorities generally, whereas most of the time I had no idea what she was talking about.

Despite the dissimilarity of our backgrounds, we had a good relationship, though—the sort that can be picked up easily wherever it left off. I looked forward to our lunch, and I got to the restaurant early. Yolande was already there at a table at the rear of the room, and I was disappointed to see that we weren't going to lunch alone—there was a man with her. He had his back to me, but I knew from Yolande's fact—her glowing face—that this was Peter. Then the man got up and turned around, and I found myself shaking hands with Roger Curwell.

I might have guessed. If the ministry had been smaller, or if we had had fewer contacts with the public and consequently fewer visitors to the building, I might have suspected that Yolande's Peter could be on the staff somewhere, and that that was why she was there. But it was too late to think of that now; there was nothing for it but to sit down. As I did so, Yolande made some comment about coincidence. Peter had just told her, she said, that we knew each other. Then she added by way of explanation that she hadn't meant to confuse me—she called Curwell "Peter" for no better reason than that she liked the name.

I longed for the floor to open up and swallow us. It was days since I had had any proper sleep, and I wasn't sure that I could cope with the hour that lay ahead. I must at all costs keep my own counsel and watch my step so that Yolande didn't learn anything from me that she didn't know already. I glanced helplessly at Curwell, and was rewarded with one of his most brilliant smiles. As if reading my thoughts, he suggested that he have a drink with us and then leave us to lunch alone: he was sure we must have a great deal of catching up to do. I nodded agreement with this excellent proposal, but Yolande wouldn't consider it for a moment. This was a special occasion, she said. I had been wanting to meet Peter for months.

Curwell caught my eye and gave me a small, attractive, conspiratorial wink—a man obliged against his will to indulge a woman's fancy. In no time, our lunch developed into a game: each of us talking in generalities and wondering, I'm sure, how much the others knew. I thought of the sick wife that Curwell had spoken about to the General. Was that his legal wife, or was it Yolande, or had a sick wife been invented? If it were Yolande, was she seriously ill, and if she was, did she know, and suppose that she was keeping the knowledge from Curwell? I looked at her carefully, but it was impossible to guess the state of her health from her appearance—she had always had pale skin, and dark rings under her eyes. As for Curwell, had he told Yolande that he had been fired from the ministry? If he had, he certainly wouldn't have told her why, nor that I was primarily responsible for his departure.

Curwell saw to it that I had a miserable meal: he was enchanting to me throughout. He consulted me about the food and wine, and although I cannot now remember what we settled on, I know I was grateful that rationing simplified the choice. I wanted more than anything to find out where Yolande was living and what she was doing with herself, to establish some sort of link between us that I could follow up later, when Curwell wasn't there. I had the feeling that if I lost touch with her again, I should lose touch for good, and that is exactly what happened. Today, I don't even know whether she is alive. I tried any number of approaches, but Curwell saw through all of them and he blocked (charmingly) every question I asked. He was so gracious with his picayune revenge—I had cost him his job, he would cost me my friend—that he made it impossible for me to press for answers that were not readily forthcoming, and the one time I did press, I was so clumsy and abrupt that Yolande exclaimed: "Don't answer her, darling! I never do when she nags." I did learn that Mr. Cookham's London office had been closed, and that Yolande was about to move from her present apartment (wherever that was), to one within walking distance of her job (whatever that was). "People really ought to walk *more* to work, don't you think?" she asked.

It was not until the end of the meal that I realized I wasn't suffering from embarrassment, but disappointment. Yolande had never given me much of a picture of Peter, and I had filled in the gaps for myself, turning him from the kind of man she had, into the kind I wanted. It was hardly fair to blame Peter for being handsome, casual, and clever, instead of as I had imagined him: reliable, humorous, and good.

It then occurred to me that I had no reason to watch my step. Yolande would not be affected by anything that I or anyone else could tell her about Curwell. People are capable of love at all sorts of levels, and, while it lasted, this rickety level of theirs had to be included.

When the bill for our lunch came, it was on two checks. The waitress recognized that we were from the ministry, and it was the custom for each staff member to pay his own way. Curwell picked both checks up, and when I expostulated, he reminded me—with another of his splendid smiles—that Yolande had said this was a special occasion. If I paid for myself, I might forget it, and he wanted me to remember. They were both beaming at me—one radiant, the other mocking—and I said that put that way, how could I refuse? I certainly wanted to remember, I said. And I have.

Wedding Garment

In spite of writing through a large part of seven nights, I didn't manage to tell Linda very much of Yolande's story. I did, however, make time to tell her all of another and shorter one. It concerned my wedding dress.

I don't suppose I would have thought to tell her had not one of her circle of friends proposed to marry rather than return to school after Christmas. The announcement raised a whole new series of telephone topics for the group, ranging from the wisdom (or folly) of such a step (all the boys, I noticed, were against it), to the number of bridesmaids, and the flowers recommended by Washington's leading florist as the most satisfactory for a bride's bouquet. Linda, notwithstanding the example her parents had set her, was wildly romantic about marriage. Her beautiful eyes would swim with emotion at the smallest reference to rings and vows and white satin trains, and of course she wanted to hear about my marriage and in particular what I had worn. She was disappointed when I told her that my wedding garment had been a blue and white pinstripe suit, but she understood that if one marries in wartime and in a foreign country veils and orange blossom and a row of bridesmaids are really not very appropriate.

The blue and white pinstripe suit was the most valuable of my possessions, apart from my engagement ring, when I came to America in the spring of 1945. It had been designed for me by my father's tailor, a taciturn man who did not think the female figure a suitable substructure for good clothes. Mr. Gunn—that was the tailor's name—Frederick Gunn—did not normally make clothes for women at all, and the only reason why he was prepared to do so in my case was because my father was an old customer, and I had promised not to wear the suit on the English side of the Atlantic. I intended to be married in it, in New York.

It was really a beautiful suit. The material was soft and lightweight, and yet it had a firmness that gave body to the style we chose—or rather, to the style that Mr. Gunn said I was to have. This was very plain—a single-breasted jacket with three buttons, narrow lapels, pockets that were proper pockets and a skirt that was slightly flared. What made the suit particularly valuable was that in 1945, clothing was strictly rationed. The suit took up two-thirds of a year's coupons (I couldn't possibly have suggested to Mr. Gunn that he go easy on the material) but when I finally saw myself in it, I thought it was worth every one of them.

Charles was then with the U.S. Air Corps in the Pacific. When I learned that there were some 60,000 European wives of G.I's awaiting shipment to America, I applied myself to finding a British-Government-approved job in the States so that a mere fiancée could cross the Atlantic ahead of, rather than after, all those legal wives. It took me twenty months of effort (the British authorities, understandably, had more pressing matters on their minds than helping me to marry Charles), but I made it in the end. I got a job with British Information Services on the 48th floor of Rockefeller Centre, and a room in what seemed to me after wartime London an enormously luxurious 57th Street hotel.

My English friends assumed that I would do a lot of clothes shopping now that I was in a country where clothing wasn't rationed, but although my new job paid better than my old one, I had lost the habit of buying clothes. I did invest in a few small items, but I had my beautiful suit (unworn) hanging in my hotel closet, and for the rest I thought the few old clothes I had would do until I knew where and in what climate a demobilized civilian geologist might want to live.

Charles reached New York eight months after I did, and we were married on a December Sunday morning, in St. Thomas's Episcopal Church. No members of either of our families attended the ceremony, but one of the newsmen at B.I.S. lent his apartment for a party for us, and someone managed to find some champagne.

What I remember best about that day was my sense of relief. Getting married had been no end of a bother, what with Charles's Point System and the fact that he speaks Japanese, and me being liable to British National Service until I reached the age of 51. But all the necessary permissions came through, and the wedding ceremony felt as peaceful as dropping the right pieces of a jigsaw into place. There was even a rightness about the New York weather—we had snow, but not heavy snow, and the sun shone on streets that were crisp and very clean.

We spent our honeymoon in Pittsburgh. This was not because Charles couldn't think of a more likely honeymoon spot, but because the Geological Society of America meetings were being held there, and Charles, on terminal leave from the Air Corps, was looking for work. We stayed four days and then, job in hand, returned to New York.

A month later, one of my British Information colleagues who had been on home leave when we were married, telephoned her congratulations. She wanted to know what I had worn, and I described in some detail Mr. Gunn's lovely suit. After she had rung off, Charles asked why I had said all that, and I told him that women were always interested in what other women wore, particularly to their own weddings. But, Charles said, that wasn't what I had worn at all. He remembered very clearly how I had looked in church that Sunday—starry-eyed in a little black sweater and mottled brown-and-mustard skirt. I then remembered very clearly too. I owned a dusty black sweater and rumpled brown skirt that had been with me through many air raids, and I had put them on at daybreak that morning while I packed, made tea, and paid my bills at the women's hotel.

It was very difficult for Linda to accept that any bride could forget to dress for her wedding. Well, I hadn't had any bridesmaids to remind me, I explained. I thought she would be amused at my chuckleheadedness, but on the contrary, she was shocked. She said she had heard about the frigid British and she might even have seen them in the movies, but she had never expected to meet one.

Last Chance

After Linda left (I don't think the hospital ever found out what had caused her stomach pains) a twelve-year-old girl was moved in. Her name was Nona Smithson, and she could hardly have been less like her predecessor. Nona was the ninth child (she was correctly named) of a devout and delightful Catholic family, all of whom felt personally concerned with the automobile accident that had smashed Nona's jaw and covered much of the rest of her in cuts and bruises. She had been riding in the passenger seat of a friend's car when the driver took a curve too fast and the car overturned. The accident was inexcusable, as indeed ours had been, but I noticed that neither the Smithson family nor the covey of priests who came to visit spent their time on regrets—they simply made a point of showing up and being there. Nona—a slender girl with a long face, placid blue eyes and long, straight, ash-blonde hair—can never have felt neglected.

With her jaws wired together, Nona of course couldn't talk, although she could make sounds. Conversation between us was much more difficult than it had been with Linda, but as some member of her attractive family was almost always in the room, I didn't try very hard to communicate. Instead, I dozed and communicated with my own memory—

reminding myself of another member of a large family whom I had known—a Derbyshire boy named Last Chance.

If Last Chance had been born after my father became rector of Whately, Derbyshire, he would not have been given that name. My father was fussy about names, and if the one chosen for a child seemed to him unsuitable, he would refuse to proceed with the christening ceremony until another was selected of which he could approve. I do not know whether the clergy of the Church of England are entitled to behave in this autocratic manner, but no one, so far as I remember, ever questioned my father's right to. Armistice Jones, born one November 11, was transformed on the chancel steps of our tenth-century church into James, while Zeppelina Worsthorne, who arrived at the time the newspapers were full of the visit of a German airship-designer, became at short notice merely one more Mabel.

Nothing, however, could be done about Last. His name had been given to him when he was three weeks old by my father's predecessor, a clergyman bolder than my father at tempting Providence. He was Harry and Evangeline Chance's fifteenth child (as it turned out, he really was the last Chance), and when he was about eleven, he came to work at the rectory, cleaning our shoes before his school day began, and our knives after it ended—our table knives had steel blades that were not stainless. Partly perhaps because Last was small for his age and no taller than I, he never would tell me his exact age. I was eight, and a girl, and he despised me on both grounds.

Harry Chance was a 'butty', that is, an elected supervisor, at the Whately coal mine. The family was well off, though from Last's appearance one would never have guessed it. No new clothes were ever bought for him—his trouser legs had to be turned up and pinned to keep him from tripping over them—and his mother rarely cut his hair, with the result that he went about looking like a neglected Skye terrier. At that time, young people in England could leave school and go to work as soon as they became fourteen, so in a large family there were apt to be several full-time wage-earners. Harry Chance had growing sons who cut coal, and daughters with good jobs in a neighboring woollen mill. The system meant money, but it also meant that Evangeline's housework was never done. Since the mill operated from seven in the morning until five in the afternoon, and the mine in shifts around the clock, some member of the family was always sleeping, or wanting dinner, or waiting in a tub of hot water before the kitchen fire for his back to be scrubbed clean of coal dust. Not that Evangeline let the situation get her down. She just kept going around the clock, like the mine. She scrubbed and polished and laughed and cooked, putting relays of meals (dinner, breakfast, or whatever, according to the dictates of the stomach of the consumer) on the table and removing the empty dishes as fast as they were swept clean.

The Chances lived in New England, a very ugly section of Whately built by the colliery company at the turn of the century on the floor of a valley, where for much of the year it was covered by a pall of black smoke. The New England houses are built of brick, in short, straight rows, like bumps on a bar of cooking chocolate. The Chance house, being at the end of a row, had an open view to one side, with extra windows facing on to a slag heap. (For a couple of years it had an open view in front as well, caused by an earthquake. The ground subsided when the roof of the worked-out mine beneath collapsed, and the house opposite the Chances' front door fell down.)

No New England house, not even an end one, was big enough to accommodate a family of seventeen, but by the time Last was born, several of his older brothers and sisters had married and moved elsewhere. None went far, however. The Chances were clannish. They had no wish to leave the neighborhood.

One might have expected that a fifteenth baby would be made much of by the rest of his family, but spoiling children was not the Chance way. Love abounded in their house all right, but it was a buffetting love, the kind customary to a crowded litter. When Evangeline, a big, jolly woman with a round red face, placed some loaded platter or other on the kitchen table, there was nobody to see that Last got his share except Last himself. If he did not snatch at the dinner as soon as he saw it, bigger hands than his would snatch it first. This was fine for Last's brothers and sisters, all of whom were outsized, strong, and well able to hold their own, but for Last, it meant a continuous battle for survival. He longed for the time when he would be fourteen and therefore, he thought, a grown man, released for good from the family teasing about his small size, and capable for the rest of his life of a man's job down the mine like his brothers. With Last, the usual problem of aging was reversed: he was like an old man imprisoned in a child's body. Even when I first knew him he did not walk like a child, but scuttled about fussily, as if he were already middle-aged.

Being a Chance was something to live up to. The family reputation was high, not only at the mine and the mill, but also in the community. Evangeline sang in the church choir, never missed a meeting of the Mothers' Union, and, with daughters and daughters-in-law to help her, cut the sandwiches, sliced the pies, and kept the tea-urns filled at every village party. Harry and his sons, shift-work permitting, played on the cricket and soccer teams, judged the racing whippets, and could always be relied upon to fetch and carry, hang up decorations, and take them down again. With the exception of Last, who was not a joiner, the Chances were stout supporting pillars of any number of local organizations.

In his determination to seem bigger and older than he was, Last's job with us was a help to him. For a short time each day, nobody could deny that he was a working man. He had the same high standards of accomplishment as the rest of his family—he polished our shoes until his scowling face was reflected in them, and ran our knives up and down the brown-powdered knifeboard as if his life depended on the disappearance of their stains.

My mother always noticed Last's work, and made a point of telling him from time to time how much she appreciated his services. She put a cookie tin on the shelf above the knife-board, and this was exclusively for Last's use. It was a large tin, and many things besides cookies went into it. When we had individual mince pies for dessert, one would be placed in a paper bag in the top of Last's tin. Sometimes there would be candy, or a piece of cake. If there wasn't anything else (besides cookies), an apple or an orange would go there. Last never mentioned these gifts to my mother, though he knew who they were from: it is not a Derbyshire custom to say thank you. He was, however, conscientious about them. The first thing he did when he came to our house in the afternoon was to look in his tin and see what was there, but not until he had finished his work would he stand beside the knife-board and eat his goody, using a cookie or two as a chaser.

I wanted very much to be friends with Last—he was the only other child I saw at the rectory—but he rejected all my overtures of friendship. By emphasizing our similarity, I merely emphasized his closeness to childhood, the thing he was trying hardest to ignore. Over and over again (I was both persistent and optimistic) he made clear to me how little he thought of my toys and games. My father electrified my train, with batteries for power, and I spent hours making scenery for it to run through—the batteries made impressive freight-yard buildings. But when the work was finished, Last would not even look at the result. The gardener put a swing up in the horse-chestnut: Last would not ride. I can only remember one occasion on which he almost unbent and became a boy, and that was when I took him to see Apocrypha on her nest.

Apocrypha was a peahen. She belonged to my mother, as all our peafowl did, but Apocrypha was more sociable than the other birds and her great charm for me was that she would let me stroke her neck. It was a beautiful neck, thickly covered with brown and shot-green feathers (it is pea*cocks*, not the hens, who are brightly colored). While I stroked, Apocrypha would stare and swallow, and make appreciative noises that were part gulp, part chortle.

Apocrypha was an inquisitive bird, who liked to know what was going on. For several seasons after she had acquired her mature plumage, she did not nest, contenting herself with picking her way about our garden and looking the opposite way whenever an admirer tried to attract her attention by staggering in front of her with his magnificent fan raised. The other peahens always nested in the apple orchard, back from the road under the trees, but when Apocrypha finally built, she chose a spot close to the road, at the top of a ridge of ground that bounded our property. There were bushes growing on the ridge, so that when she was seated on her nest she was not exposed, but if one knew where to look, one could easily see her from the outside, and she had a fine view of everyone that went by. With her neat, though dumpy, body and her correct, stylish coronet, Apocypha on her egg reminded one of a contented, gossipy aunt. She was the kind of bird who would have added a porch rocker to her nest if she had known how.

One spring morning, after I had been trying for years to persuade Last to play with me, I asked him if he would care to come and see Apocrypha on her nest. To my delight, he said he would. As soon as the shoes had been shined to his satisfaction, we set off for the orchard, Last bustling along with his usual nervous walk, and me telling him, as I followed, that he must step quietly and firmly, so that the nesting birds would hear without being startled.

Apocrypha seemed pleased to see us. She looked us both over, first with one eye, and then, swinging her beak around over her back, with the other. Last smiled. He asked in a whisper if I thought Apocrypha would let him stroke her neck? I said I didn't know, but that my mother never touched a sitting bird. At that moment (somewhat to my relief, for I didn't enjoy disappointing Last), the church clock struck a quarter to nine: time for him to go to school, and me to breakfast.

Last never came to see Apocrypha again. When I proposed it, he replied that it was no fun if she couldn't be touched, and that, now that he knew where to look, he could see all he wanted of her from the road.

But if Last did not welcome my friendship, he greatly welcomed my father's. They were closely bound on two counts: they built fires together (open coal fires were our only means of heating), and my father never used Last's Christian name. He called him Chance, as if he were already a man. "Chance!" he would shout down the long stone corridor that connected the front part of our house with the kitchen quarters, "My lump, please."

This lump was a lump of coal for the study fire, the construction and lighting of which was a daily ritual at the rectory throughout the winter months. No one was permitted to touch this fire except my father and Last, though others, such as myself, might look on. The ingredients were a few dry sticks, one sheet of the *London Times,* and a lump of coal that measured approximately 10" × 12" × 8". Using a match, a hearth-brush, a pair of bellows, and a captured Napoleonic sword, my father and his Ancient (Last) started a fire of such proportions that even by American standards the study was overheated. The job was never begun until mid-afternoon (when Last was on his after-school stint at the house) so that the room was not warm until dinnertime, but after dinner, my father was assured an evening of complete privacy. Even if one could stand the study's temperature, there was nowhere to sit down. The only accommodation free of books and papers was a small sofa wholly occupied by my father, and the brocade-covered top of a piece of furniture intended both for seating and for a fireguard. This was made of wood faced with asbestos, and it fitted against the fireplace like an E with the middle bar removed. The top was about a foot wide and eighteen inches high, and although it was firmly upholstered, it was not welcoming, being too close to the source of raging heat for safety. The brocade was badly scorched, and there were any number of charred holes in it through which tufts of black hair unattractively protruded.

I often watched the lighting of the study fire. The procedure fascinated me. First the middle of the grate would be swept clean with the hearthbrush, so that any unburned pieces from the night before formed a rim, like a volcanic crater. Within this crater, *The Times*, bunched loosely, would be emplaced, and the sticks laid carefully across it. Next, the lump of coal would be added, its ends supported by the sides of the grate; sometimes the center of one long side had to be propped up by the point of the sword, the handle of which was wedged against the center of the fireguard. Then a match would be struck and put to *The Times*, after which Last would begin pumping the bellows. From this point the game was on: no two fires burned alike. Depending on the amount and strength of the down-draft from the chimney, the dryness of the sticks, the size of the lump, and other variables, my father and Last might produce a good fire in a few minutes, or after a half-hour fight. Last always manned the bellows, moving the nozzle from side to side or up and down as he was ordered, while my father wielded the sword, using it, when necessary, as a poker. On some days, it seemed as if victory was touch and go. For minutes on end not a spark would be seen and great clouds of blue smoke would fill the study, but my father and Last always won. In all the years I watched, I never saw a fire go out, or a second match be needed.

Once a fire was started, the lump required constant supervision. As it burned, it would slip and turn over, and my father would have to manoeuvre it into a fresh position. Sometimes the lump would fall out of the grate altogether, an event that would do nothing to improve the condition of the surrounding brocade. If the lump fell while we were across the hall having dinner, my parents and I, hearing the familiar crash, would leave our food and run. There cannot be many women alive today whose meals have been as frequently interrupted by a father's swordplay.

In all this activity, Last lent able support. He was quick with the bellows, and calm when, on occasions, flames leaped unexpectedly or naked steel slipped. I was not jealous of his privilege: the study was a man's world, and its incensions were men's work. Indeed, one of the few times when my father became seriously annoyed was when women invaded his fire-making—if, for example, my mother forgot to tell a new cook not to touch the study grate or prepare coal for it. My father considered it criminal extravagance to break coal into handy-sized pieces, though this was not on account of cost. Coal was extremely cheap in our neighborhood, particularly if one bought it, as we did, at the pit-head, and 'led' it ourselves. Once a year Mr. Earwaker, a carter who was also, appropriately, one of the church bellringers, made enough trips with his horse and cart to fill a brick coal-pit in the rectory back yard with great slabs of coal. Sheets of tarpaulin would then be placed over such of the coal as we did not expect to need during the next two months or so. From the pit, the slabs were transferred by wheelbarrow to a small coal-room attached to the house, and here the cook would chop up most of the big chunks. When I asked my father why he objected so strongly to the cook's method of preparing coal, he took me out to the coal-room and showed me the dust that her daily assaults created. Then he reminded me of the length of time it takes a lump of coal to form. There was no need to remind Last that coal was valuable. He probably knew as little geology as I did, but respect for coal was born in him. To Last, coal was not only the means of keeping warm, it was his bread, his ambition, and even perhaps his calling.

A week or so after I had taken Last to see Apocrypha on her nest, my parents took me to London for a vacation. While we were gone, Last and two boys from a village in the next county broke into the orchard and stoned Apocrypha to death.

The village was stunned. Nobody knew what to do. The gardener, in whose charge the birds had been left, telephoned to us in London, the local newspaper printed the story, and a representative of The Royal Society for the Prevention of Cruelty to Animals, a parrot-faced man in a peaked hat, came over from Derby and assured Harry and Evangeline that my father would be certain to take the matter to Court. By the time we came home, Apocrypha had been buried and her egg given to another peahen, but the foster-mother had rejected it. Last was home in bed, where, having told his family what he had done, he refused to speak to anyone. The Chances were beside themselves in their bewilderment. Last's behavior was so far beyond their understanding that, perhaps fortunately, they decided he had gone out of his mind and they did not punish him. Instead, they urged him not to worry: all that had happened was that he had gone mad.

The first thing my father did on his return was to send for the R.S.P.C.A. man, and inform him, in a brief interview, that he had no intention of suing the Chances. (The R.S.P.C.A. man was much disappointed: coalminers are notorious for their devotion to animals, and Apocrypha's was the first case in our neighborhood he had ever had.) Next, my father received a visit from the two boys who had accompanied Last into the orchard. Their parents came with them. This interview lasted longer, and during it an offer to pay damages was made and refused. Finally my father sent a message to Last: would Chance bring him a suitable lump?

As soon as he was told this, Last got up and came over to the rectory. He picked out a particularly good lump and carried it to the study where, in silence, he and my father built a fire. As soon as it was going well, my father asked Last if he had killed Apocrypha. Last said yes, sir, he had. Then my father asked if he had persuaded the other two boys to help him with the operation. Last again said yes, sir. After a pause while he adjusted his sword, my father remarked that there occur in every man's life regrettable episodes that can never be satisfactorily explained or fully understood. One way to deal with such lapses is to observe the widespread distress they cause, and having done so—in detail—the next step is to regard the matter as closed. He proposed to follow this course now. Very soon Last would be fourteen and leaving our services to become a miner. Until then, there would be shoes to be shined, knives cleaned, and lumps fetched as usual.

It was at this point, my father said afterwards, that Last broke down. He was to become fourteen the next week, he explained, the great day was as near as that, but he had learned from the colliery officials that he could never become a miner: he was too small. He could have a pit-boy's job if he liked—helping with the ponies, filling lamps, feeding the canaries (canaries were used to detect the presence of gas)—but what use was that to a *man*, especially a man named Chance? The terrible facts cascaded forth. When it seemed that Last had no more to say, my father suggested that the two men take a walk down the valley. The senior churchwarden of Whately Church happened also to be the manager of the Whately mine.

How matters were satisfactorily explained to the Chance family I do not know. They must have been eager to have the incident closed and forgotten, and no doubt this eagerness helped them to accept whatever reasons my father supplied. All I was told at the time was that Last would be leaving the following week to go to the mine, and that in the meantime I must not mention Apocrypha's death to him. But of course I did. "Whatever made you do it?" I wailed. "Whatever made you do it?"

Last did not answer, as I should have known he would not. The cruelty seemed all the worse to me because it was Last's cruelty, and when the next week the longed-for fourteenth birthday arrived and Last left the rectory, I made no attempt to say goodbye to him, or wish him luck.

Not long after that, I left the rectory myself to go to boarding school. With so much new to think about, I mostly forgot Apocrypha and what had happened to her. The news from home was about a new mine-shaft that was being sunk. Shortly before I came home for my first vacation, my father wrote that he and I were to have a chance to go down the new sinking. (My mother would not be coming, I knew. She was not one who found the inside of the earth stimulating.)

It turned out that we had to descend in a bucket that dangled on the end of a cable—there was to be an elevator, called a "cage", like the one we were accustomed to in the old shaft, but it had not yet been installed. The bucket was large enough to hold five men in addition to my father and me, but because it was so much smaller than the cage the shaft was intended for, we swung about a good deal, and bounced on the air.

We were very glad of the oilskin coats and hats we had worn, as always, but never seemed to need before—water dripped on our heads and shoulders all the way down. When we hit bottom, the bucket canted over at an angle on the uneven ground. Fortunately, with the aid of a well-timed last-minute shove from Mr. Hughes, the assistant manager of the mine who was escorting us, I came out on top.

The new sinking was a damp, chilly area about twenty feet across, not yet painted but already brightly lit. We scrambled clear of the bucket and moved as quickly as we could to the perimeter, so as not to hold up work. A dozen men, using shovels and their hands, were busy gathering the rock and dirt that had been loosened earlier by blasting. Others were drilling holes for the next blast. Still others were busy at tasks I could not identify, connected, I supposed, with the lighting, ventilation, and signalling systems, or just stood by. Opposite us, one of the standers, but with an expression of fierce concentration, was

Last, dressed like the other miners in strong boots, trousers, and a tin hat, and holding an odd-shaped tool. I noticed that this tin hat was new and shiny, and that his trousers fitted him. I also noticed his tenseness and excitement—he looked like a man with a responsible job to do that he knew he could do well. When the bucket we had vacated had been filled with rubble, it was raised just far enough off the ground for a small man (Last) to drive underneath and scrape the mud and stones from the bottom, using his tool as a scraper. While he worked, Mr. Hughes explained that if a good-sized pebble were to fall off the bucket when it was near the top of the shaft, it could kill a man standing at the bottom, even if he had his tin hat on.

My father, who believed that one should never speak to a man on a job if one could avoid it, ignored Last's presence, and Last ignored mine. Nevertheless, after the bucket had swept aloft, I tried to catch his eye. I longed to speak to him, to tell him how glad I was about his job, and especially that I had forgiven him for Apocrypha's murder. I understand now, and perhaps, seeing him so happy, I understood dimly then, why he had done it. All his runt-sized life, Last had dreamed of becoming fourteen, and consequently a big man and a coal-miner, never suspecting that it was possible for a Chance of New England to achieve one of those three states without the others. Suddenly he learned, or thought he learned, that he was permanently excluded from the brotherhood below ground. His frustration and rage turned, not against their cause, but against the people he thought he could hurt. Somehow the rectory family, with my father's respect ("Chance" instead of "Last"), my mother's consideration (the cookie tin), even my nagging, unquenchable devotion, meant more to Last than the casual teasing affection of his own home, where his feelings went unrecognized. But when he wanted to harm us, we were not there, and all he could see when he haunted the road outside the empty rectory was Apocrypha on her nest.

I could not, of course, have put such thoughts as these together coherently as I stood looking at Last in the bottom of the sinking, but even if I could have done so, I had no opportunity to speak to him. Last stayed on his side of the area, and Mr. Hughes would not let me cross over. We caught the next bucket back.

I wondered what Last would do after the cage was installed in the new sinking and there was no further demands for the services of a bucket-bottom-scraper. My father said that, so far as he was aware, the law concerned itself only with the age of a workman, not his dimensions, and that Whately colliery's objection to an undersized miner would probably be overcome, once that miner proved himself diligent and conscientious. And that apparently was what happened. In due course, Last was transferred from the bucket to another underground job. There was never any more talk of employing him to lead ponies, fill lamps, or feed canaries.

I must have run across Last in the village from time to time when I was at home on vacations from school, but the only clear recollection I have of seeing him again was after I was grown up, during my father's funeral. We were in the churchyard, and the rector of the next parish was reading the closing prayers against the sounds of rain and wind. I happened to look up, and saw Last, standing in the rectory meadow outside the churchyard wall, looking through an opening between two stones. He wore a cap several sizes too big for him, and under it his face was a pudding of grief. He watched us dazedly, as one might watch people one had never seen before. He looked unutterably alone.

As soon as the minister finished praying, I went over to the gap in the wall. I don't know what I expected to say or do when I got there, but Last did not give me the opportunity. Before I could reach the wall, he darted away. He must have been twenty by then, but he scurried up the meadow with the same nervous, middle-aged step that he had had as a small boy. I never saw him again.

The Underground Banquet

As it turned out, I never visited the new sinking again, although if it hadn't been for the ruptured appendix of a man I will call the Earl of Sherwood, I certainly would have. The occasion of which the Earl's appendix, coupled with my father's insistence on keeping his word, robbed me was the colliery company's dinner to celebrate the sinking's opening. It was held at the bottom of the new main shaft.

I usually managed to wangle a trip down the mine two or three times a year. My father and I would join a small party of three or four escorted by the assistant manager—we were not allowed to wander about on our own below ground, the way we could above. Our visits always took place at an hour when we would not interfere with a shift changeover, and when the traffic on the cages and subterranean roads was mostly coal. Our journey would begin in Mr. Hughes' office, where the adult members of the party were fitted with Wellington boots and oilskin coats and hats belonging to the company, and I put on similar clothing of my own that I had brought from home. Then we would file over to the Lamp Room, to be given safety lamps. These burned oil, and everybody going below had to carry one.

The cages were built in three tiers, each tier being divided vertically by a steel partition, on either side of which two mine cars or ten men

(I think it was) could stand. The floors of the tiers were laid with narrowgauge track, so that the mine cars, the trucks in which the coal travelled from the coal-face to the shaft base, could be brought to the surface easily. The cages were open at either end except for a pair of stout chains. We were always put in the center tier, with me in the middle for greater safety, and as soon as the spaces beside, above, and beneath us had been loaded with returning empty mine cars, a bell clanged and we plunged into the earth.

The operator normally dropped the cage at sixty feet per second, but if MEN RIDING showed on his indicators, he slowed the speed to half that. All the same, to inexperienced passengers, thirty feet per second felt fast. It was perfectly dark in the shaft except for the tiny lights of our lamps, and windy too, as if we were at sea in a gale. At the end of about a minute, the cage began to slow down, and suddenly it jerked to a stop at the shaft bottom. Around us was a white-painted cavern, crowded with men and mine cars, from which white-painted tunnels led off in different directions.

At first, our eyes were dazzled. The electric light down the mine seemed much brighter than the daylight above. We stepped off the cage, and while Mr. Hughes talked with some of the miners, I watched the pit-boys form the empty cars into trains. When a boy had linked three or four cars together, he would climb into the front one, and by engaging a clutch, attach the train to a moving cable that lay between the rails. Then off they would go with a jerk, jogging down one of the white tunnels at the speed of the moving cable. Meantime, trains loaded with coal had been lined up ready to go aloft. As soon as the cage had been filled, another bell clanged, and the whole structure roared upward, sucking a pillar of dust and candy wrappings after it.

We always walked the two miles to the coal face; visitors were not allowed to ride in a train of empties. The road we took—one of the white tunnels—contained two narrow-gauge tracks, and it was just as brightly lighted as the shaft-base. Wooden props held up the roof, which was strung with telephone and electric wires. We walked on the hard, even ground between the tracks—we couldn't walk between the rails of a track because of the moving cables. Mr. Hughes strode along, and we followed in single file. In my Wellington boots I would soon have been left behind, except that every time a train approached, he would stop and wait for it to pass, and I would catch up.

My visits to the mine took place so long ago that I find it difficult to judge what size the tunnels and the mine cars actually were; they looked larger to me than they would now. I think the tunnels must have been about twelve feet wide, and they were certainly high enough to give a tall man head room. The cars perhaps measured four by two and a half feet and were four or five feet high.

We always made several stops between the shaft bottom and the coal face. The first of these was at an engine-room where, whatever the time of day, we were given thick mugs of strong, hot tea. A while later, we stopped to admire a fossilized tree trunk—our coal seam, we were told, had once been growing in a part of Sherwood Forest. A third stop was at ventilation doors. There were three sets of these, built across the whole tunnelling system, making up two "air locks", and beyond them the air pressure was higher, as the level of water is higher beyond locks in a canal. When we pushed through the door of a lock, we became momentarily deaf, recovering our hearing just in time to lose it at the next door.

Beyond the air locks, our tunnel took on a new aspect. It wasn't white any more, or nearly so brightly lighted, and the ground was less smooth. Now we could walk the ties if we wanted to, because instead of cables to pull the trains, there were ponies. There were about two hundred ponies at the mine, and in order to keep them in good health and free from blindness, they were worked in rotation, two-thirds living below while the others rested above ground in stables and meadows that adjoined the colliery yard. The ponies were quite tall, at least they seemed tall to me, and they were very strong and sure-footed, though I think the trains they pulled were shorter than the ones drawn by the cables. Each pony wore blinkers and brightly-polished harness, and some had on bells and colored ribbon rosettes as well. The boy in charge walked beside his animal, because there wasn't room enough between the pony's back and the tunnel roof for the boy to ride.

Everything always seemed to happen abruptly in the mine. Our walk along the tunnel stopped suddenly, at a point where the tracks ended and the tunnel opened out into a shallow bay. The roof was lower here, and in the rock immediately ahead of us was a shining belt of dark silver: the coal.

In the Thirties, at least in our mine, coal was mostly cut by hand. The miners worked in teams of eight, each team electing its own head man or 'butty', and arranging which job fell to whom. Some swung picks, others shovelled up what the pickers had knocked out and loaded it into cars which the boys brought as near to the face as the tracks allowed. The whole job proceeded methodically and with a kind of deliberate grace—if it hadn't been for the sweat on the miners' bare torsos, one might have supposed that this wasn't back-breaking work. The men wore trousers, heavy boots, and tin hats. All of them were thickly caked with coal dust.

The first time I saw the coal face, the team we visited was taking a rest (they were drinking cold tea out of bottles) and the butty invited me to hack out my own piece of coal. I took his heavy pick and swung it at the silver wall. Nothing happened. The butty laughed and said something to my father. Then, handing me a small hammer, he led me off up a ladder to another level where a man was lying full length on a shelf of rock, working at a much narrower face of coal. When he saw us, he grinned and moved over, making room for me on the shelf. I squeezed into the space, and crawled along until I was level with the face too. Then, using my hammer (the hard picking had already been done), I dug out a small, very shiny piece of the beautiful coal. Lying there with my treasure, I felt, I remember, not only extremely pleased with myself, but also extremely safe, though actually I suppose neither I nor my father's half-naked parishioner can really have been particularly safe where we were.

Except for the area under our tenth century church, all the coal within profitable hauling distance of the pit-head had been removed, which was why the colliery company had decided to sink a new shaft nearer the coal face. The dinner to celebrate its completion was a luncheon really, scheduled to take place in the middle of the day, but everybody referred to it as a dinner, and although I did not actually receive an invitation, to my great delight I was asked: my father was told that he might bring me with him if he wished.

My excitement over this event wasn't so much that I would be eating dinner at the bottom of a mine shaft, nor that there would be champagne, a beverage that I liked very much but was only rarely allowed. It was because this was the first time I had been asked to a party that wasn't a children's party. English children aren't, or at least they weren't then, normally included in adult festivities, and the invitation made me feel very grown-up. I suppose the colliery company had thought of asking my mother, but they knew she didn't much care for the insides of the earth.

Besides my father and me, only one person unconnected with the colliery was bidden to the Sinking Dinner. This was the Earl of Sherwood. Over the Derbyshire county line, thirty miles away in Nottinghamshire, were five large adjoining estates, known collectively as the Dukeries. The members of these households were so good about lending their patronage to charity bazaars, foundation-stone layings, and the distribution of diplomas that no event of importance took place in the neighborhood without the presence of one of them. Those with a flair for such work—naturally, some were better at it than others—were engaged months in advance. Unfortunately, the organizers of the Sinking Dinner didn't think of the idea in time to allow themselves a choice of patron. The Earl of Sherwood was all there was left.

Lord Sherwood lived alone in a very beautiful house tucked away in a wood. He was a poor public speaker, which is why he wasn't invited out more, and his interests were health movements and growing his own tobacco. Whenever he ran across my father at some function or other, he would press upon him a generous tin of strange-smelling, stringy strips, to which my father, normally a courageous man, never quite had the nerve to put a match.

As soon as Lord Sherwood received his invitation to the Sinking Dinner, he accepted it. Ever since we had known him, he had been wiry and strong (he spent a great deal of time taking impressively long walks), so it was a surprise when, two days before the event, word came that he had been whisked into hospital for immediate surgery.

If our village had been located in any other district of England, I suspect that the Sinking Dinner would have been held anyway, earl or no earl. As it was, the date was postponed for a fortnight (Lord Sherwood had said he was sure he would be all right by then) to the exact day and time at which my father was contracted to perform a wedding.

Unfortunately my father did not see the Sinking Dinner in the same light that I did. After writing a letter to the organizers declining with thanks the redated invitation, he regarded the matter as closed. When I did not, he explained to me that although one day was just as good as another for getting married, he had contracted to do a job of work on a particular day at a particular time, and he would alter his plans only for an extremely good reason—the collapse of Lord Sherwood's appendix not being one.

The solution seemed to be for me to go to the Sinking Dinner alone. My father saw no objection to this, provided my hosts suggested it without preliminary promptings from me. Neither my father nor I expected the organizers to remember so vital a matter when they had much else to do, and our surmise proved correct.

On the day of the dinner, Lord Sherwood turned up at our house shortly after breakfast, carrying his customary gift of tobacco, and looking as craggy and fit as an old tree. The manager of the mine called for him around noon, and immediately afterward my father had lunch, so as to be in good time for his wedding. At one o'clock, the hour at which I judged the roast beef, Yorkshire pudding, and champagne were being served below, my mother and I sat down to the cold mutton, rice pudding, and shandy being served above.

It was late in the afternoon when I next saw my father. He had called at the mine on his way home. The dinner had been very successful, he told us, except for one thing. When the champagne was opened, it was found to be flat. To the relief of the organizers, Lord Sherwood drank water—his doctor's orders—and as a result he was the only diner not taken ill. The others decided to toast the new sinking anyway, in the flat champagne. "So you see how glad you can be that you missed it all," my father said, grinning. It seemed that when the party was over and the Sinking Dinner diners returned to the surface, the champagne effervesced as it was supposed to do, but in, of course, different containers.

The Corn Dolly

What with my paralyzed tongue and Nona's wired jaws, communication between us required patience and perseverance. We waved and pointed and wrote each other notes, but after our visitors went home each evening, we mostly gave up and settled for television. Our tastes in programs differed—Nona had a stronger stomach for violence than I—but we found we both enjoyed anything that had spooks and ghosts and witches in it. The interference of the supernatural in any form had us with our breath bated and our eyes glued to our tiny rented screen.

Nona's family kept us well supplied with books and magazines in our favorite subject, and even Nona's priests contributed, although their offerings tended to stick with black magic and be spoiled by moral conclusions. My mother, not to be outdone by persons of the Roman Catholic persuasion, came through with a number of hair-raising tales which, if not rooted in Protestantism as she claimed, at least owed their origins to history. The one that Nona liked the best (perhaps because it concerned a girl of about her own age) was called *The Day of the Corn Dolly*.

The name of the girl in *The Day of the Corn Dolly* was Alexia Reston-Brown, and she really had nothing in common with Nona except age. Nona was bright and resourceful, whereas Alexia was so slow that her parents sent her to a special school for backward children. The school was expensive and oldfashioned, but owing to the character of the women who ran it, extraordinarily successful. It comprised twenty boys and girls between the ages of eight and thirteen, and it belonged to Edith Taylor, who operated the school at her family's old home, and Manor House, Ault Ash, Derbyshire.

Miss Taylor, a short, round woman with a faded pretty face, genuinely loved her pupils, and she tried to provide them with the kind of life she enjoyed herself—there was plenty to eat, plenty of playtime, not too much classroom work, and a great deal of listening to Miss Taylor read aloud. Every evening of the school term, the students would gather in the Manor House's draughty drawing-room and hear about Hercules or Hannibal or Ulysses or Lord Nelson or Billy Budd. The literary fare was varied, but it always described courage in the face of danger and victory over fearsome odds. In a sweet voice trembling with emotion, Edith would read of people rescued from drowning, or dragged from burning buildings, or of the British flag planted where it had never been planted before. She did not look particularly brave herself, but once embattled, she could be formidable. She fought the County Board of Education over her school's accreditation (she lost), and the rector of Ault Ash over the Corn Dolly's participation in the annual Harvest Parade (she won).

Since I knew the Corn Dolly story already, my mother adapted it freely for what she felt would be Nona's benefit. She left in most of the bits likely to arouse goose-pimples, and glossed over the solider facts. This made for odd gaps, and I thought the story as I had originally heard it was better. Mine began with Edith Taylor's two battles with authority: first with the Derbyshire Board of Education, and then with the rector of Ault Ash.

The trouble with the Board of Education was its firm refusal to rec-ognize a school whose Principal hadn't earned any of the customarily accepted diplomas, while the trouble with the rector was his refusal to recognize any good in a pagan ritual. Edith couldn't do anything about her lack of diplomas, but she came up with some rousing arguments in favor of the Corn Dolly. Far from its being an encouragement to drunkenness, concupiscence, and unseemly brawling as the rector averred, the Dolly, which had been carried in procession through Ault Ash at Harvest-time for at least eight-hundred years, not only attracted tourists but also earned the village an asterisk in the County Gazetteer. The story was that any prayer offered to the Dolly while she was borne through the streets would be answered within twelve months—being a goddess of fertility, the Dolly was especially partial to the prayers of young girls. Edith admitted that some people used the observance as an excuse to consume more alcohol than was good for them, and the neighborhood was apt to be noisy during the night following the parade, but she believed in encouraging public interest in folk-lore and tradition, and she did not think that people who want to drink, shout, and concupisce require reasons for doing so.

Edith had lived in Ault Ash all her life, and her opinions carried weight. In spite of the rector, who was not a Derbyshire man, the Corn Dolly continued to have a place in the Harvest Parade, although well to the rear of the Christians. The Dolly's appearance varied from year to year according to the skill of her weavers. She was made of oats, barley, wheat, and maize picked from the last shocks to be harvested, and her face was carefully painted on the side of an upturned china bowl that had been bound to her neck with raffia. After the parade, the Dolly was thoroughly dowsed with water, and then carried back to the farm from which she had come. She would spend the winter in one of the barns, nurturing within her the promise of next year's growth. In the spring, as soon as the first shoots showed that life had returned to the earth, the Corn Dolly would be considered to have completed her mission, and she would be burned.

It was a delightful tradition, and the rector would have had no objection to it had it not been for a curious odor of evil with which the Dolly was surrounded. Somewhere, somehow, back in village history the Corn Dolly had come to be associated with all sorts of devilment. Any piece of careless behavior, from illegitimate births to traffic accidents, was attributed not to the shortcomings of man, but to the willfulness of the Corn Dolly. When the rector pointed this out to Edith Taylor, all she said was that if you give the devil his head on one day in the year, he is more likely to leave you alone on the other three-hundred-and-sixty-four. The rector, well aware of Edith's devotion to Ault Ash and Ault Ash customs, only hoped that this extraordinary philosophy was not a part of the curriculum of the Manor House School.

Of course it was. Each year, before taking her charges to see the Parade, Edith made a point of telling them about the Corn Dolly and her supposed mysterious powers. What Edith did not mention was that as a young girl she had frequently prayed to the Corn Dolly herself. She had asked, not for the blessings of husband and fertility, but for her own school. A great many Harvest Seasons went by before her prayer was answered, but finally her ailing parents died and set her free to live her life instead of theirs. The Manor House was left jointly to Edith and her elder sister Mabel. Edith and Mabel agreed at once that Edith should have the house for her school (Mabel didn't want the place—she had escaped from Ault Ash years before, to go on the stage.) Success came late in life to both of them, quietly in Edith's case, loudly in Mabel's. Edith was forty-four when she started her school, and Mabel forty-nine when she first appeared as the wicked Miss Warhead in *The Wicked Miss Warhead,* the most popular children's serial on British television.

The sisters admired each other very much. Edith's devotion to her school astonished Mabel, and Mabel's nationwide fame astonished Edith. Three television sets were installed in the Manor House so that everybody could have an uninterrupted view of Mabel's program, and on Friday evenings Edith's heroic readings were replaced by the stirring adventures of Miss Warhead. The Manor House children knew that Wicked Miss Warhead was their Miss Taylor's sister—several of them had met Mabel when her occasional weekend visits to Ault Ash coincided with term-time. Knowledge is not self-integrating, however, and as the children rarely saw Mabel and often saw Miss Warhead, the television character was much the more real to them of the two.

Wicked Miss Warhead concerned the adventures of an elderly lady pilot employed by a foreign power to undermine the operations of British Missile research. Each week, Miss Warhead almost succeeded in pulling off some coup or other ruinous to the British effort, and each week she was foiled by a group of children who cooperated with, and sometimes did better than, the London Metropolitan Police and Scotland Yard. Miss Warhead had an advantage over her pursuers in that when she wished to do so she could alter her size, becoming larger or smaller than real life. This gave the trick-camera people something to do, and it also made the arms of the law look less foolish when Miss Warhead eluded them, as she always did. Everybody in *Wicked Miss Warhead* (except wicked Miss Warhead) was noble, brave, and self-effacing, though a trifle incompetent because the B.B.C. saw no sense in catching their most popular criminal before the ratings drove them to do so.

Mabel Taylor was perfect casting for the part. Short like her sister, she was thin and wiry, with her father's pale eyes and beaky nose. By the time she became a television star, Mabel had spent twenty-five years in provincial repertory, turning out one flawless bad-hat of a spinster after another: fortunately, the plays popular with North-of-England audiences almost always contained a Mabel Taylor part. What made Mabel so suitable for Miss Warhead, however, was not so much her long apprenticeship in the theatre as her true nature. While Edith thought all young people charming, Mabel thought them brats. Mabel had, therefore, only to express her feelings in her face and there, with little further effort, was Miss Warhead. She even wore her own clothes for the role—an old tweed suit (good in its time) and a hard, unbecoming little hat.

Alexia Reston-Brown of course knew all about the legend of the Corn Dolly, and she was also an avid watcher of the Warhead programs. The year she was twelve (Mabel's series was then in its second season) she decided that the time had now come to treat the Corn Dolly seriously, and to pray to it and enlist its help. It so happened that Mabel Taylor decided almost the same thing. She did not propose to pray to the Corn Dolly, but she was too old a hand in the entertainment world to suppose that *Wicked Miss Warhead* could provide her with employment indefinitely, even though her success was such that there were *Wicked Miss Warhead* dolls on sale—short, skinny figurines in tweeds and hats—and *Wicked Miss Warhead* records. Properly handled, a pagan deity let loose once a year in an English village ought to be good for at least half a dozen programs. Accordingly, Mabel put the idea to her director, and then invited herself to Ault Ash to refresh her memory. "I shall drive down on Saturday morning," she wrote to Edith. "Don't look for me before the show in case I have car-trouble and am delayed. I'll see you at home for dinner."

That was all the preparation Mabel made. Alexia Reston-Brown made considerably more. In the privacy of the broom-closet at the top of the back stairs, she wrote and memorialized a prayer. After the work was done, she learned from Edith that to be effective, prayers to the Corn Dolly had to be offered at the exact moment at which the supplicant was beside her. Realizing then that a long prayer would not do, Alexia cut out everything except one sentence: *Oh Goddess Corn Dolly, please give me a magnificent and dangerous dragon to slay.*

This was a rather vague request, but it was the best that Alexia could do in the circumstances. Praying was not a habit with her—her parents, who were both psychiatrists, deplored it. But in her slow and bumbling way (Alexia was a fat girl and this made her slowness seem even slower) what they had to say on the subject tied in nicely with what she heard said at Ault Ash. At home, what counted was to be brainy. At school, what counted was to be brave.

Alexia was well aware that her parents were clever and that she was a disappointment to them, but she was also well aware that they loved her, and she longed to please them. One day, Edith's reading caused her to say that bravery was just as good as, if not better than, a good brain. Alexia clutched at this like a drowning man at a straw. Perhaps after all there was a way to make her parents happy that did not depend upon writing and spelling and adding up. Alexia didn't find it at all difficult to be brave. She never minded getting into a fight and when she did she could usually hold her own, even with boys. Things that frightened other children—the magical powers of Miss Warhead, for example— never scared her. She was always the first to push forward when something that required courage had to be done—a stray dog removed from the play-yard, a hornet squashed on a window. But bravery that one could equate with a good brain required more than hornet-squashing. She must get her hands on something really important—preferably with death in it. So far as she knew, there was no place near Ault Ash where anyone was likely to be found drowning (and so need rescuing) and there had not been a fire at the Manor House in Edith's lifetime— she had inquired. It was then that Alexia thought of the Corn Dolly. The Dolly might be out of practice, and if her parents were right about the ineffectualness of prayer, nothing could come of her efforts. On the other hand, her parents might be mistaken. They had been wrong already over the eight schools to which they had sent her before alighting on Ault Ash, and if they were wrong now, the Corn Dolly might give Alexia just the opportunity she needed to make them proud of her.

This was why, armed with her one-sentence prayer, Alexia elbowed her way to the front of the crowd at the corner of High and Church. She would be closer to the Corn Dolly there than she could be anywhere else on the parade route.

There was a Harvest Tea in the Community Hall later on, but Miss Taylor's children were not invited to that. Everybody was pleased to see them lined up along the street, though. Edith noticed Alexia's pushing and shoving for a particular place but she did not say anything. The afternoon was, after all, a holiday.

The procession started in good time, moving out of the Ault Ash Elementary School playground (Mixed Infants Entrance) punctually at three. The Silver Prize Band from a nearby colliery town led off, and then came detachments of Boy Scouts, Girl Guides, and members of the Saint John's Ambulance Brigade. There were trucks from the Volunteer Fire Department, and four floats depicting scenes of local history—one concerned Mary Queen of Scots who had been imprisoned in a country house a few miles outside the village, and another the childhood of Florence Nightingale: Miss Nightingale's family came from Derbyshire. But as soon as the last of the floats had gone by (the girls in their thin dresses looking pinched and cold and in need of their tea), the atmosphere of the parade changed. The marchers loosened up and no longer tried to keep in step. They laughed and talked with each other. A group of Morris Dancers in costume shouted comments to the crowd, and a quartet of male singers persuaded everyone within singing range to sing with them. Very soon the parade lost formation and the road filled with people in fancy costume. Alexia noticed witches and gypsies and a girl in a ballet skirt who threw flowers from her hair into the crowd. There were a clown on stilts, and a man in a lion's head— this was the Corn Dolly's parade now, not the Christians' Thanksgiving. The watchers on the sidewalks opened beer bottles. The procession slowed to a crawl. Somewhere to the rear a firecracker went off.

Alexia saw the Corn Dolly a while before it reached her. She was high in the air, tied at knee-level to a horizontal pole slung between the shoulders of two men who stood side by side at the front of an empty hay-wain. The wain was drawn by two gaily-dressed cart-horses, and as the men swayed with the animals' movements, the figure between them dipped and rose. The Dolly was about four feet tall, with a thick cylindrical body made of dark yellow wheatstraw, and thinner cylinders, bent at the elbows, for arms. Her hands were made of wheat-ears, and a frill of barley made a skirt long enough to hide her feet. She had rows of threaded maize for a necklace, and a plaitedstraw hat, trimmed with oats. She was all grain except for her head and face—the upturned china bowl on which were painted large, very blue, wide-set eyes and a firm, bright-red mouth.

Alexia had expected that the Corn Dolly would be splendid and terrifying, and that she might, when she saw her, be too frightened to pray, but there was nothing alarming about this figure—it was tawdry and curiously familiar; like an old toothbrush. Alexia waited until the hay-wain was directly in front of her, and then she spoke her words, clearly and loudly, her eyes fixed on the Dolly's expressionless face. There was so much noise that she was sure nobody could hear what she said, and yet, as soon as she had spoken, she felt her breath catch and her blood race, as if some force outside herself had responded, and given her power.

The Dolly's hay-wain was the last vehicle in the procession. Behind it walked the owner of the farm from whose fields the last sheaves had been gathered, and with him a seedsman, a thatcher, and finally (in long dresses and crowns of flowers) a group of village girls.

The parade over, Edith Taylor gathered up her charges and walked them home. The smaller children had been pushed and jostled enough so that they were tired of the afternoon's fun. They were much more interested in last night's Miss Warhead episode that they were in the

Corn Dolly. Alexia stumped along in silence, listening with half an ear to their remarks about Miss Warhead's escape from the police in the back seat of a school bus. Edith said: "I've got a surprize for you all this evening," and Alexia, out of her newfound power, smiled kindly. Edith's surprizes usually meant nothing more than ice-cream for dinner.

Mabel Taylor had watched the parade from another part of the village. She had arrived in time to join the Manor House party, but she had not done so—she would see all she wanted to see of her sister's schoolchildren later in the day. She was disappointed in the Corn Dolly Parade. Although the procession had all the color and racket that she remembered from earlier years, the Dolly wasn't stylish enough for export to television. Mabel sensed ill-will and foreboding emanating from the stiff yellow body, but how much of that was because she expected it and looked for it? Would anyone not raised in Ault Ash sense it too?

After the procession had passed her, Mabel took her car in to be greased, and then she walked over to the side door of *The Green Man*. The bar wouldn't be open until six, but Mrs. Walker was already pouring tea for her friends—hot black tea, generously laced with whiskey.

One of the charms of the Day of the Corn Dolly was that social barriers were relaxed, and one drank and visited with people one never drank and visited with normally. Mabel paid several other calls in the village before she started for home. Her progress took time (a hometown girl who is also a television star calls for opening up a bottle) and it was nearly half-past five before she pushed open the door that led from Ault Ash High Street on to the Manor House bowling-green. This route was a short cut to the back entrance, and by taking it one avoided the front lawn where Edith's children usually played between tea and dinner.

The bowling-green (nobody played bowls there any more) was a soft, rich lawn somewhat wider than a tennis court, which had been carefully cut and rolled for two centuries. It was surrounded on three sides by a

stone wall, and on the fourth by a hedge with a gate in it. Beside the
gate lay a pile of stones and a small, half-built rockery that Edith had
been working at, on and off, for years. The gate led into the Manor
House vegetable garden, beyond which was the kitchen entrance to the
house.

What with the long drive, the procession, and the refreshments she
had been plied with during her calls, Mabel felt tired and less alert than
usual. She was already on the bowling green, with the heavy door from
the High Street closing behind her, before she realized that the locale
of tea-to-dinner play had altered since her last trip home in term-time:
Edith's children were at play *here*. A desultory ball-game was going on,
and a fat child whom Mabel did not think she had seen before was
standing by herself beside the rockery.

Everyone stopped and stared. Mabel smiled and introduced herself:
Mabel Taylor, their Miss Edith's older sister, down from London for the
weekend to see the Corn Dolly Parade.

The children continued to stare. Then a small, sharp-faced boy with
a head that seemed a size too large for him replied: "You're not Miss
Edith's sister. You're Miss Warhead."

Mabel inwardly sighed. This had happened before (it was one of the
drawbacks to wearing one's own clothes and very little make-up at
work) and when it did, one had to humor the customers. "Quite right!"
she answered cheerfully, "How clever of you. Did you see my program
last night?" She grinned Miss Warhead's grin. "Then you know why I
thought it would be wise of me to leave town for a few days."

She began to walk across the grass towards the gate in the hedge. As
she did so, she saw the children draw together, as if for protection.
Well, good, she thought. They're not sure whether I belong in a story
world or a real world, and they're afraid—all except that fat girl by the
rockery.

The fat girl said: "Do they know you're here?"

"They?"

"The Police. Scotland Yard."

Mabel laughed Miss Warhead's laugh. "Of course not. I don't want to get arrested, do I?"

The girl's face seemed to light up. She moved quickly over from the rockery to the pile of stones. She shouted: "Stay where you are! Quick, everybody—catch her before she changes size."

It was Mabel's mistake, of course, to run, but she had never played Miss Warhead for longer than one sentence without a script before, and for a brief moment, before she became alarmed (she was, unfortunately, not entirely sober) she was annoyed at the turn events had taken. She would, nevertheless, have been quite all right if Edith had finished her rockery-building and cleared away the pile of surplus stones.

✳ ✳ ✳

Walking home to tea, during tea, and out on the bowling-green after tea, Alexia seemed to see the Corn Dolly everywhere she looked. I mustn't sleep from now on, she thought, in case my dragon comes in the night . . .

And then, quite suddenly, there it was, on the bowling-green. Not exactly a dragon, but certainly the opportunity for courage that she had asked for—wicked Miss Warhead in person, out-numbered, unarmed, and normal-sized. Alexia knew exactly what to do and what orders to give. She threw the first stone.

The stone hit Mabel precisely where it had been aimed—in the face. Alexia saw Miss Warhead pause, reel, and put one hand up. She looked angry, bewildered, and then bloody. The other children laughed and quickly joined the new game. There were plenty of stones in the rockery pile for everybody.

When Miss Warhead dropped to her knees and rolled over on the grass, it seemed clear that there was no more danger: she was destroyed at last. Presently she stopped moving and moaning, and then Alexia felt free to leave the group and run indoors. As she ran, she babbled prayers of gratitude to the Corn Dolly. It hadn't really been difficult at all—just a matter of recognizing evil when one saw it, and keeping one's head. And now everybody was going to be so proud of her—her parents, the school, Miss Edith, the Police, Scotland Yard. . . .

Alexia didn't feel she could face public acclamation immediately—she needed to spend a little more time alone with her success and the Corn Dolly. Avoiding the playroom, she ran upstairs to the broom closet, where, among the mops and buckets, she knelt down. Her heart was racing. If the B.B.C. invites me to make a television appearance, she thought, I wonder if Miss Edith will let me have a permanent wave?

Presently, she heard footsteps running. They came up the stairs and past the broom-closet. Alexia did not move. They would find her eventually, and when they did, she would be ready for them—cool and calm and ready for adulation, like Hercules and Hannibal and Ulysses and Lord Nelson and Billy Budd.

Time Lucy Went

Early in my stay in hospital, I was asked if I would permit groups from the University Medical School to examine me. My paralyzed tongue was, it seemed, of professional interest—nobody before me had had one and lived to enjoy it—if enjoy is the word. Thanks to our car's seat-belts, I was alive instead of dead, and everybody wanted to take a look. (Seat-belts had not been mandatory equipment long enough then to show how satisfactorily they save lives.) I agreed, though I might not have done so if I had realized that part of the drill for me would be spending several hours with my mouth full of sharp-edged cameras.

The doctors and students who came to see me were courteous and impersonal. What absorbed their attention was not me, but the damaged container I was living in: my body. They discussed this object freely, as if it were an ancient, formerly valuable, but now discarded garment. "There's nothing wrong with the voice-box!" one exclaimed, using exactly the reproving tone I had heard my mother use to a dressmaker who wanted to throw out a suit that still had a few months' wear left in its jacket. Meanwhile (cowering inside) I longed to replace the best that medical science could offer me with a visit from Dr. Hwfa Morgan, though if I had been able to do so I would surely have died.

Dr. Morgan was the General Practitioner in Whately, the small isolated Derbyshire community in which I grew up. He really knew very little about medicine, but his incompetence was accepted because he knew a great deal about people's need for affection and sympathy, and he always seemed to have time to sit down and offer them that. He was a gentle, friendly, and obliging old man and he was a great believer in leaving as much as possible to nature. (When nature failed, Dr. Morgan comforted the bereaved with the unarguable maxim that Heaven is a better place than this is.) Riding about the village on his ancient bicycle, with its hard little saddle and high handle bars, Dr. Morgan would dismount at once if he saw a child in tears or an old woman carrying a heavy bundle. I remember meeting him one day and announcing, "Dr. Morgan, it's my birthday and it's *raining!*" At once, a look of deep concern came over his face. He asked me gravely how old I was, and when I told him, he tilted my face up to the stormy sky and said, "Look-you! It does not rain at all. It is just the heavens weeping for joy because a little girl is six years old."

Hwfa Morgan was Welsh (he pronounced his first name *Hoo*-vuh) and he had a marked Welsh lilt to his voice, but he had lived in the area for so long that everybody thought of him as a native. He was a pillar of the Revivalist Chapel, and he had a real feeling for local mores and village history. Not long after my parents moved to Derbyshire at the end of the First World War, my father received a letter from the War Office asking for the names of any soldiers who were buried in the village churchyard. The letter went on to say that if the surviving relatives so wished, the government would provide memorial headstones for the graves. Most of the men in our county had spent the war either on their farms or in the nearby coal fields, and my father thought it unlikely that there would be any names to send in. When he consulted Hwfa Morgan, however, the doctor assured him that a large number of soldiers lay buried in the churchyard, and what a fine idea it was of the Government's, look-you, to offer headstones for them! Later it turned out that no one knew the soldiers' names. The graves were those of men who had died fighting in the Wars of the Roses, 1455–85.

My father did not approve of churches competing with one another, and every now and again he would invite the Revivalists to join his congregation in a combined service. I always enjoyed these occasions. The Revivalists were strong on extemporary prayer, and I used to hope that my father, who liked to stick to the book, would get shouted out of his place in it, but he never did. With his wits sharply about him and King James's language in support, my father managed to hold his own.

The most common complaint about which Dr. Morgan's patients consulted him was a variety of goitre known as Derbyshire Neck. Our damp climate, together with the water we drank, was said to be the cause of it. No one in my family ever developed this complaint, but it was so common that when Deuteronomy 31 was read in church, I used to think that Moses had been extremely tactless in his remarks to the Levites about their appearance; a stiff neck was something no one could help.

Derbyshire Neck is not painful, but it *is* ugly. The neck swells up until, in severe cases, the head looks like a small teacup set in a deep saucer. Typically, Hwfa Morgan had no remedy to offer his Derbyshire-Neck patients, but he was always ready with sympathy, and that in itself was a help. (Having grown up in Wales, he was unlikely to develop the disease himself.) The person in our village who had the worst case of Derbyshire Neck was Lucy Poole. When Lucy wanted to turn her head, she had to turn her whole body as well.

Lucy was unique in other ways, too. When I first knew her, she was a big woman in her late sixties, and, apart from her Derbyshire Neck, she was quite handsome. She was the senior member of a large, clannish family that lived in a hamlet a mile or two north of our village. Lucy's house was a gray, stone, one-story structure, built down the side of a hill. It consisted of three separate sections, which, although adjoining, did not connect on the inside, so that to go from one part to the next, one had to walk around outdoors. Because of the contour of the land, each section was on a different level. The center one was the oldest and had a walled courtyard in front of it, paved with big flagstones. On the side facing the road, the wall was about six feet high. A wooden gate opened onto the public road.

This middle section of Lucy's house dated from the eleventh century. The downhill wing was added during the seventeenth century; it was the largest, and had the best view: the two windows looked across a small overgrown garden to the valley below. Some decades later, the uphill wing was built, but even with these later additions, it was not a big house. Pooles had lived there for as long as anybody could remember or any records showed; it was thought that Pooles had built the original house. No structural alterations had been made for more than a hundred years—the latest change was made by Lucy's grandfather, who had replaced the ancient thatch with a slate roof.

Lucy and her granddaughter Patty lived in the downhill wing. Patty's mother was the only one of Lucy's offspring who did not live at home. She lived in London, and came home once a year, usually for a few days only. Lucy's front door opened directly into a low-ceilinged, good-sized room, used as a combined living room, dining room, and bedroom. Across from Lucy's big bed, there was a smaller one for Patty. In a narrow passage off the big room was a huge coal range. Beside the front door, there was a window set high up, and through this Lucy could see the boots of approaching callers as they descended the stone steps that led from the courtyard to her front door. The other sections of the house had three rooms apiece. The central section was occupied by Lucy's son Ezra and his wife and their three children. Lucy's son John and his wife and their two children shared the uphill wing with Hiram, Lucy's eldest son. Hiram was a middle-aged man with a well-developed case of Derbyshire Neck and the mind of a good-tempered baby. He used to spend most of his time sitting on the wall beside the gate, waving a battered felt hat at anybody who went by on the road. I liked Hiram the best of the Pooles, because he always had time to stop what he was doing (waving) and talk to me.

Mrs. Ezra had fixed up the smallest of her three rooms as a kitchen, but Mrs. John had none; the small room in her section of the house that ought to have been the kitchen was occupied by Hiram. It was probably Mrs. John's lack of a kitchen that had turned Lucy into the family cook. Two or three times a week, all the Pooles (including, as often as not, cousins from up the valley) sat down to a huge meal at a long wooden table in Lucy's and Patty's bedroom. On the days when Lucy did not cook, the Pooles lived on leftovers stored in cupboards that had been dug into the hillside behind the John family wing.

One might have expected from the Pooles' long establishment in the village that they would be the backbone of our small community. Unfortunately, no Poole was ever the backbone of anything. As a group, they were polite, taciturn, slovenly, and vague, and the only reason they were able to get along at all was that they clung together. None of the Pooles ever kept—or, apparently, wanted to keep—a job; all of them spent far more of the year out of work than in it. The men did casual farm laboring. Now and again, my mother, in desperation, would call on Mrs. Ezra or Mrs. John to come and help out at the rectory. They would—if they remembered about it. In the meadow below their little garden, the Pooles kept some scraggy hens and a hutch or two of hare, but these animals bore little resemblance to the excellent game and poultry that were sometimes to be seen roasting in Lucy's oven. It was generally assumed that the Pooles were more successful at poaching than at more lawful occupations; no Poole, so far as I remember, was ever in trouble with the law. Sometimes relatives helped the family out.

Lucy had a nephew who was a hotel cook in Sheffield and another nephew who had a job with the railroad in Nottingham. After visits from either of these gentlemen, the Pooles seemed to eat more frequently and the children might be bought shoes.

The Pooles were polite enough when one called there, but they did not mix with the rest of the community. In a place with a greater number of new inhabitants, there would probably have been a good deal of criticism of the Pooles' easygoing, feckless habits, and of the way they were always the last to do a job of work and the first in line when it came to free church suppers. Most of our people, however, had lived in or near the village all their lives, and the Pooles were accepted much as the weather was—not really what one would have chosen but what one had.

Lucy was something of an exception; she did not seem to mind working, so long as it was work around her own home. She strove, in a confused, muddly way, to keep the family fed and clothed, and she did not appear to resent the fact that nobody ever helped her except Patty. Since everything that the Pooles possessed was either worn out, cracked, or broken, it was difficult for Lucy to achieve what women's magazines call a gracious effect, but she did try. When one called at the house, if Lucy was not cooking she was usually to be found stabbing away at dusty corners with a worn-out broom.

North Midlanders are not communicative folk, and the Poole family were more silent than most. I never heard them converse with each other or joke or laugh, and yet the atmosphere of their home was not depressing, and I should have visited there more often if I had been permitted to. The Pooles liked to sing. None of them had a particularly good voice, but all could sing in tune and hold a part, and they knew an enormous number of folk songs of the kind that tell, in a long succession of verses, some frightful story of murder, rape, or desertion. When

I think about the Pooles, I think of them as I used to see them on one of our rare fine days. At a time when everybody else in the community was at work, Ezra and John and their wives, and such of their children as had succeeded in playing truant from school, would be sitting, with perhaps a visiting cousin or two, along the walls of the little paved yard, singing. Hiram would be perched in his usual place, waving to the passersby, but half turned, facing his relatives, so that he could sing with them. Sometimes, several songs would be going on at the same time, but the jangle was never unpleasant to hear. In theory, of course, none of us wanted any part in the lives of the worthless Pooles, but when they were singing together, they had a kind of strength and warmth and power about them that I suspect was the envy of some of the more solvent but less closely knit families in the village. When the Pooles grew tired of singing, all of them but Lucy would simply sit, waiting contentedly and in silence until she had their next meal ready.

When Patty was about thirteen years old, Lucy had an attack of influenza. My father thought that she should go to the hospital in our market town, but she refused to leave home, and since Dr. Morgan did not agree with my father ("Mother Nature is the best doctor of us all, my dear sir"), Lucy stayed where she was, tossing with fever in her big, broken bed while the family crowded in around her and ate the meals that Patty cooked for them.

Patty was a stolid, plain girl who hardly ever smiled, and she was hard-working in the way that Lucy was—no particular objection to work if it could be done around home.

My parents worried about Lucy, because she took so long to recover. Even after all traces of her illness had left her, she continued to spend most of the time either in bed or waddling nervously about her room in a greasy wrapper and scuffed slippers. For the next three years, she kept catching colds, one after another, until she became thin and sorry for herself, and the only part of her that remained unchanged was her swollen neck. Patty did the cooking and such cleaning as she cared to do, and Lucy occasionally helped her.

The summer Patty was sixteen, she acquired a beau—Sammy Keppler, the baker's nephew, an easygoing young man, who apparently felt perfectly at home in the Poole household. There was some amused speculation in the village about what the Pooles would do when Patty married and left home: Lucy was obviously not strong enough to take on all the family cooking again, it was unrealistic to expect Mrs. Ezra or Mrs. John to do it, and there wasn't room in the house for another family. The Pooles owned most of the scrubby hillside around their house, and Sam and Patty could have built themselves a place nearby if they had wanted to, but I suspect that the idea never occurred to them. I can remember only two new houses going up in our village, and the people who lived in them were not envied. With a new house, you were bound to have trouble—unfamiliar drafts, leaks, and plumbing deficiencies. Whatever the drawbacks of an old house might be, at least they were known.

That winter, after New Year's, we had a spell of unusually bad weather. My father had been to see Lucy at Christmastime, but it was February before he called on her again. When he arrived at the house, he found two dogcarts in the road outside—a sign that either the nephew from Nottingham and the nephew from Sheffield or the cousins from up the valley were visiting. It turned out to be all of them. The entire Poole clan was assembled in Lucy's room. Every inch of space seemed to be occupied, all the windows were closed, and through the open door into the passage my father could see that the draft of the big cooking range was wide open and there was a roaring fire. Close to the front door, placidly sharing a rocker, sat Patty and her Sam. Most of Lucy's relatives were singing, but this time the song was not one of the old folk tunes that we were accustomed to. It was a dirge. Mrs. Ezra and Mrs. John were keening.

My father was so astonished that at first he did not notice Lucy. Her big bed was covered with the bodies of little wailing children, who, not unnaturally, were objecting to the heat and the fetid atmosphere. Lucy herself lay propped up on two gray pillows. All that was visible of her was her head and the upper part of the wide column of her neck. She lay with her small mouth open in a round O, and through the aperture her little gray tongue could be seen flickering with terror, like the tongue of a chicken that is parched with thirst. Her black eyes fixed themselves at once on my father, but she did not seem to know who he was.

The behavior of the Pooles within the confines of their own home was no business of my father's, but he ordered them to stop singing, and they did. Then he pushed his way across the room and opened the only window that could be opened. After that, he turned everybody out of Lucy's room except Patty, and he told her to keep the place clear of relatives while he went to find Dr. Morgan.

My father knew, even while he was doing this, that his efforts were futile—that as soon as his back was turned, the clan would crowd into Lucy's room again. Later in the day, when my mother called at the house, the singing and keening were once more in progress and Lucy's window was tightly shut. My mother knocked at the door, but nobody answered and she had to come away. As for Hwfa Morgan, he listened to what my father had to say, and he promised to go and see Lucy just as soon as the family sent for him. (Local mores demanded that the doctor not call unless he were invited to do so). This the Poole family did not do for ten days, and then it was because Lucy was dead.

The funeral was a large one, and there was an all-night wake feast.

After a few weeks, Patty and Sammy got married, and Sammy moved into Lucy's rooms. With a baker in the family to keep them in fresh bread, the Pooles lived better than they ever had in the past. My father never spoke of Lucy's death, but I heard Dr. Morgan mention it once, years later, when Sam and Patty's little boy was old enough to be playing truant from school. All Hwfa said was that from the way things had improved up at the Poole house, it almost seemed, look-you, as if when Patty married, it had been time Lucy went.

Mr. McAlligator

Two of my favorite callers when I was in the hospital were the Swiecickis. Americans are accustomed to difficult or puzzling surnames (my husband has a colleague named Mary Mrose) but my family in England was sensitive on the subject. Our own name was so fanciful that we always left half of it off, out of courtesy to those who might need to recall it later. Perhaps that is why, in private, we always called our village schoolmaster Mr. McAlligator, although his real name was McOstrich. I think of him with dislike but also some respect, since he was the only person with whom I ever knew my father to have a really serious row. It was one of those rows that go so deep that when the arguing is over, nobody seems to have won, though Mr. McAlligator lost his job as a result of it, and my father kept his.

In many ways my father also respected Mr. McAlligator. He came from a Tyneside town, where he had been one of a large, poor family, and he was thin and bent in the way tall men are who have not had enough to eat during childhood. He had a big head, a jutting chin, and wide-set, angry brown eyes, but when he moved it was apologetically; he had a shuffling, sheepish walk. If Mr. McAlligator had had a first-class brain, or even a second-class one, his life could not have been the misery it was. He was feverishly ambitious, not for money or social advancement, but for learning—he yearned for recognition as a scholar.

When he was growing up, there were no free places in the better English schools for indigent boys with drive, purposefulness, and less than average ability. Nevertheless, by correspondence courses, evening classes, and Workers' Education programs, he managed to qualify as a schoolmaster—our country schools were desperately short of teachers. It never occurred to Mr. McAlligator that others might have a less fanatical reverence for learning than he did. His method of teaching was, apparently, to terrify his pupils into remembering their lessons. Unfortunately, few parents in the village wished to revise this system; they thought stern discipline essential for children, and Mr. McAlligator was admired as a man of character.

Mr. McAlligator was avidly devout, and a member of our Church Council. He never missed a meeting, voting automatically against any motion my father proposed. He disapproved (violently, as he did everything else) of everything my father did or stood for. He was shocked by frivolousness, and a clergyman who mixed faith with humor must have seemed to him frivolous to the point of blasphemy. My father believed that Jesus had, among his other attributes, a sense of humor, and he often used a humorous anecdote to make a point in a sermon, though the point itself was entirely serious to him. I think Mr. McAlligator thought of the Church as a raft for Christians to float on, while pagans had to bob about as best they could in surrounding shark-filled waters, whereas my father thought of the Church as a raft for Christians to take breathers on between swims.

Another thing about my father that infuriated Mr. McAlligator was his attitude toward political and social affairs in the community. With the local coal mine operating on a shift basis around the clock, pastoral visits to parishioners' homes were often inconvenient. Consequently, my father took to doing most of his parish visiting in the bar of *The*

Goat and Compasses, the forum for exchanging and debating news in Whately. In order to hold his own in the arguments that went on there, he had to know not only the local whippets' forms, but also what any visiting political and trade union speaker had to say. Neither duty was a hardship. The dog-racing trials were exciting, and the public meetings never dull. The village hall would be hung with bunting and slogans— FOOTPRINTS IN THE SANDS OF TIME WERE NOT MADE BY SITTING DOWN, for example—and whatever the cause, the applause (though not necessarily the vote) went to the speaker best able to keep his temper when heckled. "Daisy!" I once heard a miner shout at a trade-union delegate, "You got enough brass in your face to make a kettle." "And you," Daisy retorted, beaming, "you got enough water on your brain to fill it."

Meetings were held on Saturday nights, and the next morning the organizing committee of the political party or trade union concerned attended church, perhaps on the basis that since my father had supported their effort, they would support his. My father made a point of attending all the meetings of the more radical groups in the neighborhood, not because he hoped to make converts the next day, but because he felt any contacts based on fair play should be encouraged.

Mr. McAlligator was shocked that an official of the Church should participate in any controversy but a theological one, and tried to dissuade my father from attending the political meetings and the dog races. My father was amused to note the similarity in this one attitude between Mr. McAlligator and Mrs. Harvey-Rice, for probably in no other respect would either of them have admitted a similarity to the other.

Mrs. Harvey-Rice was a rich, autocratic, amusing old lady who was really my father's employer. Most clerical appointments in the Church of England are made by the bishops of dioceses, but some of the older livings are in private gift. This system dates back to the time of Elizabeth I, when the chaplain to a great house might also be the parish priest. Mrs. Harvey-Rice owned two livings, ours and the one in the tiny village that lay at the end of her own drive. She lived in a beautiful house on the other side of the mountains, in some of the loveliest country in England. Our bleak and rainswept countryside so depressed her that she never came to visit us, and consequently, she never interfered in the affairs of our church. Instead, she invited my parents to visit her a couple of times each year. On these occasions, my father would tell Mrs. Harvey-Rice anything about our neighborhood that he thought might interest her. Sometimes he mentioned Mr. AcAlligator. "There are people like that in every village," Mrs. Harvey-Rice said. In her turn, Mrs. Harvey-Rice would consult my father about her garden and the education of her grandson, and complain about the incompetence of the nervous, elderly clergyman who held her other living and whom she bullied dreadfully. Once she said she wished she could find someone like my father to replace him. "But nobody like me would live so near you," my father pointed out. "I know—that's what's so annoying," she replied.

When I think about Mr. McAlligator now, I wonder whether, if we had always used his rightful name, we might have taken him more seriously, and understood that a man who is violently addicted to anything, even learning, may have other violences as well. One winter afternoon, Mrs. Tunlaw, a miner's wife, called at the rectory with her little girl, whose hands she wanted my father to see. Betty Tunlaw was about my age, and was thought to be the cleverest child in the village. She had gone playing in the snow instead of attending school, and Mr. McAlligator had caned her fiercely, tearing both her hands.

My father went at once to Mr. McAlligator's house. The row that took place there lasted more than two hours, and during it my father learned that this was not the first time Mr. McAlligator had caned a girl. That evening, my father wrote to the chairman of the County

Education Board, asking to have Mr. McAlligator removed. It was the first time he had ever taken such a step.

News of the row spread quickly. In no time, the neighborhood was divided between my father's supporters and those who, while they did not altogether approve of a middle-aged man beating little girls, thought that my father interfered too much in the community's secular affairs.

Strictly speaking, of course, this was true. The village school and its organization was none of my father's business. He did not admit this, however. He blamed himself for not realizing sooner how wild was Mr. McAlligator's envy of cleverness—even the cleverness of a child.

The County Education Board took two weeks to answer my father's letter, and when they did, it was to emphasize Mr. McAlligator's industrious record, and the difficulty of finding men to teach in so remote an area. My father was told that if he wished to pursue his complaint, he must do so in writing. He would also have to appear, with Mrs. Tunlaw and her daughter, at the Board's next regular meeting.

My father, who thought he already *had* made formal complaint, ascertained from Mrs. Tunlaw that she would be willing to attend the meeting, and then he wrote formally to the Board again.

The month that followed was an anxious one for everybody. Mr. McAlligator resigned from the church and devoted all his spare time to gossiping with his supporters. He brought considerable pressure to bear on the Tunlaws. What he said to them we never learned, but a week before the date of the meeting, Mr. Tunlaw told my father that his wife could not go through with the case. The publicity and the criticism were too much for her.

So my father wrote to the Board a third time, saying that he would not be at their meeting after all. He was very much discouraged, but he sympathized with the Tunlaws. All he had had to face was the increasing loneliness of his position, while they had had to stand up to Mr.

McAlligator's hounding, and listen as village opinion swung almost wholly over to his side.

And then a very odd thing happened. The Board, without seeing my father, or, so far as we knew, anyone else from our village, appointed Mr. McAlligator to a post in a city school. Mr. McAlligator brought the news to my father himself, setting foot in our house for the first time since their quarrel began. He was in an even more unpleasant mood than usual. He said that he had written to Mrs. Harvey-Rice. "A group of your own clergy has publicly listed you as unacceptable to the priesthood," he shouted. "Did you know that? Your name is in a book— a book published by Cambridge University."

"Oh, nonsense, nonsense," my father said.

"It is not nonsense—" Mr. McAlligator cried.

"I have been in that book for years," my father said. "It was printed privately. Cambridge would never have touched it."

We did not believe Mr. McAlligator's story about writing to Mrs. Harvey-Rice, but he had done so. In a few days, my father received a letter from her—it was full of underlinings, just the way she talked. "How could any man suppose," she wrote, "that by adopting the incredible name *McOstrich* he could disguise the *Mr. McAlligator* you have talked about so often! Fortunately as I *never* answer anonymous letters, I am *spared* replying to this one. There is, however, one portion that *deeply* disturbs me. McAlligator refers to an ecclesiastical black list, a document *entirely* unknown to me until my grandson, who seems to have learned *nothing* at that school you recommended except *inquisitiveness*—" ("Good!" interpolated my father) "found a copy of it *here in my own library.* The pages were uncut—I cannot possibly be expected to read everything that comes into this house—but *your name* is there. I cannot emphasize *too* strongly how *upset* I am to find that you have been masquerading for years as a person of *integrity* and *worth!* I do not know *who* these clergy are, but I can see it was my duty *never* to have appointed you. I am an *old* woman, and at my age I *cannot* face making changes at a time when *all* my tomato plants need repotting and this new gardener I have who was so highly recommended to me has no idea whatever how to do it. You will have to *stay*, but please understand I *forbid* you *ever* to mention the matter again."

My father wrote Mrs. Harvey-Rice a soothing letter, as a result of which she must have forgiven him, for he and my mother continued their regular visits to her house. Mr. McAlligator was promoted several times at his city school, though he was never given sole charge of children again. Everybody came to like the woman who replaced him in our village, and gradually even my father returned to popularity. By the time Betty Tunlaw won the first of her scholarships, the quarrel was forgotten by almost everyone.

I didn't forget it. I was fascinated by the notion that my father had once been considered an unacceptable priest, even by a group of eccentric clergy. But whenever I inquired what he had done, my father only looked very solemn and said, "What a pity you didn't ask me before Mrs. Harvey-Rice forbade me ever to mention it again."

Ready Money

One does not, of course, expect a hospital stay to be comfortable, but mine was made much less uncomfortable than it might have been thanks to a legacy left to my mother by a man named James Teversal Reading. There were strings attached to this legacy—not legally enforceable ones, but nevertheless emotionally binding, which said that the money must only be spent on such luxuries as a prudent woman would think she should not afford. Accordingly, during the period that Charles and I were in hospital, my mother used some of her legacy to ride taxis to come over to visit us (instead of using the bus, or relying on friends to drive her), but she also filled our rooms with fresh flowers, and, when I was able to appreciate them, she brought me glossy magazines and several of those expensive picture books that belong on the coffee tables of the rich.

James Teversal Reading was not a member of our family, although he tried to be. One June evening towards the end of the last century, he asked Hester Roper, who was later my grandmother, to marry him. Hester, who was seventeen at the time, refused him for the very good reason that she had just agreed to marry my grandfather. Ready—that was the name James Teversal Reading liked to be called—assured my grandmother that my grandfather, though a worthy man, was a humorless one, and that she would have more fun if she married him instead. My grandmother admitted that there was some truth in this, but she told Ready (much as Orinthia was to tell the King in Shaw's "Apple Cart") that although he would be her first choice for Sundays and Holidays, my grandfather promised better for everyday wear.

Hester was a sensible girl as well as a pretty one, and her choice was wise. Ready never repeated his offer, and I have sometimes wondered whether, in the quirky way that eccentric people behave when they are in love, the only reason he proposed to Hester when he did was because he could be sure that she would turn him down. Her refusal made it possible for him to institute a game that lasted more than thirty years. Its rules were strict, and its success depended upon the participants' pleasure in observing them. The players were Ready and Hester and Arthur Strickland, my grandfather. Later they included the Stricklands' two daughters: my aunt Helen and my mother, Frances.

The Ropers and the Readings (Ready's mother lived with him) had houses across from each other in Berkeley Square, Bristol. Bristol, like London and Bath, has a number of beautiful old squares of row mansions, built around a central garden. Each was then a family home, with a kitchen and servants' hall in the basement, an entrance hall and dining-room on the ground floor, a drawing-room one flight up, and bedrooms on the floors above that. At the rear, there was a billiard room. (The Readings used theirs for billiards. The Ropers' was kept empty for dancing.)

The Ropers had lived in Berkeley Square for some years before the Readings moved there. When Ready's mother had settled in, the Ropers paid her a formal call. Ready was in Portugal at the time (the Readings were in the port and sherry business) and the Ropers did not meet him until he came back to England to take charge of the family's Bristol office. He was then twenty-seven: eleven years older than Hester.

Ready always said that what he noticed first about Hester were her teeth. They were small, even, and a brilliant white, and they lent an enchanting sparkle to her smile. I only remember my grandmother as an old lady, but she still had her beautiful teeth even then, and her smile was the kind that made you feel as if you and she shared a joke that nobody else was clever enough to appreciate. Hester was, I suppose, a frivolous woman: she loved chitchat and gossip. She attacked life in much the same way that a puppy does—she thoroughly enjoyed whatever happened to be going on. By the standards of her day, she was well-educated, though. When she married (at eighteen) she knew how to run a house and keep a staff of servants happy, and she could ride and swim and play the piano and speak good Italian and French.

I don't suppose anyone ever asked Hester what she first noticed about Ready. There would have been no need, because everyone noticed the same thing—his left leg ended in a stump just above the knee. Ready made no attempt to disguise his deformity—he simply had the left leg of his trousers tailored to fold neatly over the stump and tuck into a strap. Apart from his leg, which was a birth defect, Ready was a handsome man. He was tall, with a Byronic head of rich brown curls, large, amused brown eyes, and a beaky nose. Since he had never known what it was to have a complete left leg, he was extremely agile at getting round with a partial one. He had a wardrobe of crutches made of different polished woods (his evening pair was black inlaid with mother-of-pearl) and he used these with such dexterity—balancing on one while he threw his weight forward on the other—that he reminded my mother, when she was a small girl, of an excited, oversized spider.

Ready could, of course, have drawn less attention to his affliction if he had had himself fitted with an artificial limb, but that was not his style. Although not at all sorry for himself or resentful of his situation, he was not prepared to have other people ignore it. There are not many advantages to having half a left leg, but there are some, and Ready knew them all and milked them for everything they were worth. He knew precisely how far the sympathy of physically complete persons can be stretched to cover a cripple, and at exactly what moment the milk of human kindness sours. He had strong likes and dislikes, and he loved to tease anyone he met in whom he detected the smallest spring of self-importance. One of these was the Bristol Stationmaster. Ready went to London once a month on family wine business, and for some reason he never allowed himself adequate time to catch the train. Just as the Stationmaster was about to blow his whistle and wave his flag, Ready would come hurtling on to the platform, all flying arms and crutches and shouts. The Stationmaster, who prided himself on punctuality and who went through this act of Ready's every month, would turn crimson with fury, but he could hardly do other than delay the train. Ready always travelled firstclass, and the firsts were at the end of the train nearest to the station entrance, so he did not have far to go, and his fellow-passengers would be on the lookout for him and help him aboard. All the same, his behavior caused a great deal of confusion to everybody except himself. "In under the wire!" he would cry happily, waving to anyone he saw on the platform, as he fell into a seat.

What was Hester's charm for him? Her looks, her enthusiasms, her lack of sophistication, or the fact that she was never in the least sorry for him? All of that, perhaps. Ready was never unpunctual where she was concerned—his dashes in under the wire were never used on her. But if anyone kept Hester waiting—if there was any small delay in an arrangement he had made to accommodate her—Ready would fly into a rage out of all proportion to the cause. It was as if he recognized in someone else's shortcoming the annoyance that he himself quite often caused others.

They were small enough, the arrangements that he made for Hester—concert and theatre tickets, reservations at restaurants—but over the years, there were any number of them. This was the game that they played with their friendship, and its locale was chiefly the house in

Clifton (a Bristol suburb) to which Hester and Arthur Strickland moved after their marriage. Ready came to lunch with the Stricklands at one o'clock every Sunday, and in the afternoon the three of them—with, later, the two little girls—would walk at the zoo, or the botanical gardens. Ready thus became a quite close approximation to Hester's Sunday and Holiday husband—when it was Christmas or Easter or anybody had a birthday, Ready would be there, and between times there was the circus and the flower show and the chamber music series that he promoted every winter in Bristol's Colston Hall. Without him, as Ready had warned, Hester's life would have been much flatter and more sober.

My grandfather's role in this picture—one far too peaceful to be considered a drama—was one of complete acceptance. He and Ready never became close (all their lives they referred to each other as Mr. Strickland and Mr. Reading) but I am sure it never crossed my grandfather's mind that Ready might be seriously in love with his wife, nor that his association with Hester could in any way threaten his marriage. This is where the rules of the game came in: the players understood what their vows involved and what their responsibilities were, and it didn't occur to them to question the precepts that they had been taught were acceptable to their station. There was, for example, the matter of the articles of bigotry and virtue. These were jewellery, silver, and china—items that it was not considered proper for a man to give a woman to whom he was neither married nor engaged. Ready loved to give presents, but he was careful never to overstep the bigotry and virtue boundary, though he must have been tempted to (and, one thinks now, why not?). All the time he knew Hester, Ready had a standing order at a florists to deliver a box to her every Friday, and twice a year, in the spring and fall, a dozen pairs of white, gray, and lavender gloves in Hester's size and assorted lengths would arrive from London. And the presents didn't stop there. One of my mother's earliest recollections of

Ready are a hansom cab stopping at the Strickland front door, and the tall, insect-like figure climbing awkwardly out, loaded down with crutches and packages. "This is a Goes-Inta. You throw this part up, and when it comes down, if you've got a steady hand, it Goes-Inta that . . ." "These bonnets are for everybody in the house under ten . . ."

But the best of Ready's presents was a long-term one, which began when my mother was about fifteen. It was then that Ready began inviting Hester and one of her daughters to spend a week with him in London every spring. Like everything else connected with Hester and Ready, the project was planned well in advance (Hester went every year, the daughters alternated) and it was kept strictly within the rules of course: it had Arthur's full knowledge and approval. Arthur was, indeed, almost as pleased about these invitations as his ladies were. His job (he was President of a small bank) did not permit him to take anything more than three weeks in August for his vacation, and all his married life he had spent this with his family in furnished rooms at the seaside, in Aberdovey, Wales.

The daughter whose turn it was for the London week spent months preparing for it. Ready provided the best that the social season had to offer, and the girls were determined to dress appropriately for every event and be a credit to him. The three lunched and dined at the smartest restaurants, they went on sightseeing and shopping expeditions, and to the theatre every night, with supper somewhere afterward. The ladies stayed at Brown's Hotel in a suite with its own bathroom (Its own *bathroom!*): Ready put up nearby, at his club.

The week was not without its drawbacks. The girls were always so excited that they spent much of the time battling headaches and upset stomachs, and as the London days progressed they became more and more exhausted. Ready, who made all the choices and decisions without consulting them, never allowed time for resting, and Hester, who could have assured them an occasional pause, never wanted one: she had just as much energy as he. Ready, of course, made no demands on Hester, but he expected the girls to take in whatever he showed them, and to talk about it intelligently afterward. He knew London well and he loved to show it off. (Because of Ready and my mother's memory, I know where fig trees grow in Trafalgar Square, and where the window is in Whitehall that is never decorated for Royal Processions because it was once the door through which Charles I stepped on to the scaffold.)

It was always the girls' hope that nothing would go wrong with Ready's advance planning, because if it did he would lose his temper and make a scene. The smallest breakdown would set him off—a table for tea at Rumplemyer's not available at the time promised—the non-arrival of a taxi-cab. Hester never minded these delays or the rumpus that Ready made about them, but the girls suffered agonies of embarrassment.

The daughter left behind—the one whose turn to go to London it was not—had a good time, too. She had her father to herself for a week. The quiet, charming Arthur Strickland adored his children, and my mother's recollection of her weeks with him on her own is full of contentment. A good deal of time was spent reading Hester's daily letter, answering it, dining out, and sitting up late at night talking. My mother never remembered asking Ready for advice, but she frequently consulted Arthur. ("Would you marry Henry if you were me? I have to marry someone, I think."

"How do you like his father?"

"Oh, his *father* wouldn't do at all."

"Then probably Henry won't either. People are apt to take after their parents as they grow older, you know. You watch Henry the next time he's here. Depend upon it, he'll be taking quizzy looks at your mother. . . .")

The London weeks continued until my mother and my aunt married, but that didn't happen until they were in their middle twenties. Ready never invited Hester alone, because of course she would have refused, and it was one of the rules of the game that she must never be put in the uncomfortable position of having to say no.

Ready continued to have Sunday dinner with the Stricklands, though, and to accompany Hester and Arthur on their walks to the zoo or the botanical gardens. His presents of gloves and flowers continued, too. With her daughters married and gone, Hester had more time for him than she had had in the past, and she began trying to give him advice—to persuade him to slow down and take life more calmly. "One of these days, you'll kill yourself, scurrying the way you do," she told him, and that is exactly what happened.

He was sixty-eight, and the Bristol Stationmaster he had enjoyed teasing had died long before. The successors (there had been several) were busier men and less considerate of the behavior of one lame, elderly man. Ready was making one of his in-under-the-wire dashes one morning when the whistle blew and the train began to move. He continued on as he had always done, but the train gathered speed, and when he reached the door of a firstclass carriage, there was nobody in it to give him a hand and pull him aboard. Ready was dragged between the open door and the edge of the platform, and when they finally stopped the train and pulled him free, he was dead.

His will was simple. Apart from a few small legacies to family servants, and the Berkeley Square house to his younger brother, Ready left two-thirds of his estate to Hester, and one third divided equally between her daughters. (Hester's share also included twelve Coalport cups and saucers, and twelve tiny silver spoons. Bigotry and virtue were all right once the donor was dead.)

Hester, for all her chuckleheadedness, was astute when it came to money, and she did well with Ready's legacy. She invested most of it in a summer place with its own beach and good waterfront land near Aberdovey, and the rest she spent on small luxuries and extravagances (she cancelled the semi-annual gloves but kept on the weekly flowers) that she would not otherwise have thought she should afford. She impressed on my mother and aunt that Ready, she was sure, intended that his money be used for extras and fun—it should never be dissipated on necessities or good works.

Another generation comes into the picture now—my own. All through my childhood, and particularly after Hester's death, my mother's Ready money lay in my background like an Aladdin's Lamp. Only my mother could conjure up the genie, and her rules about doing so were just as strict as any that Hester had observed. The Ready money was banked in a different account from the one my mother shared with my father, and she would never divulge how much there was in it, nor admit ahead of time how she intended to spend it. I remember though that my parents and I went as Ready's guests to Portugal and North Africa and Paris and the Norwegian fjords, and there was one time when my new bicycle was stolen the first week I had it, and my mother discovered (miraculously) that there was just enough Ready money in the account to pay for a replacement.

In the fifties, after she was widowed, and after she had moved to Washington, D.C., there was a financial crisis in England. The Chancellor of the Exchequer blocked the movement of sterling, and although my mother was quite willing to accept restrictions on her small pension, she was outraged when she discovered that the regulation also applied to her Ready money. I had always known my mother as resourceful and good-humored in whatever situation she found herself, but that changed. Tampering with her Ready money touched an intimate and desperate chord and turned her into a woman with one topic of conversation. Nobody had ever come between her and her Ready money before, and she was determined that they were not going to do so now.

My husband and I bore my mother's complaining for several days, and then we said that since neither of us had any influence over the British

Government's decisions, perhaps the best thing for her to do would be to write to the Chancellor of the Exchequer direct, and explain to him what her problem was.

My mother thought this was a splendid idea and she cheered up at once. I wish I could have seen her letter. It went out from Washington within twenty-four hours of our conversation, Special Delivery, Airmail, and overweight. My mother's handwriting was large, and she liked to use a wide nib, bright blue ink, and heavy paper. She expressed herself easily—letter-writing was never trouble to her—and she scattered capital letters like seeds as she wrote, using them in place of punctuation. My husband doubted that my mother's letter would ever reach the Chancellor's desk, but I thought it might, if only because his clerk might decide to allow him some relief from the customary run of ministerial mail. I never expected she would hear anything more, though, and for three and a half months, she didn't. Then a formal reply arrived from the Chancellor's Principal Private Secretary. In view of my mother's remarks, to which careful consideration had been given, the Secretary was instructed to report that my mother's account was being transferred as it stood to the United States.

My husband and I were astonished, but my mother treated the news as no more than her due. When I insisted on being given some idea of what her letter had said, she explained agreeably: "All I did was tell the truth. I told the Chancellor about my war job," (In 1942, my mother had lied about her age and driven a dump truck at Aldermaston Air Force Base), "And I said I would gladly die for England any time, but I couldn't *live* for my country, particularly in America, without Ready Money. I pointed out that the British Government would not have to support me in my old age or pay my doctor's bills or the cost of burying me, and that it was Improper and Unfair in view of all those savings— I said I planned to be expensive in my old age—to keep every penny of my Ready Money as well. I told him a little about Ready and his crutches and the train accident but not much—he's a busy man. I said I knew he would understand and put everything right for me, and he has."

Perhaps the Chancellor had a stubborn and independent mother of his own, or perhaps he was impressed that a woman of nearly sixty should have risen at 4 a.m. for months on end in order to help the Americans build Aldermaston Airfield. Or perhaps it was simply that, with her predilection for capital letters, my mother's remarks about Ready Money reached the Chancellor as remarks about ready money— pocket-money, ready cash. Certainly as far as the national budget was concerned very little was involved, and perhaps the Chancellor just felt in the mood to respond to such a lavish outpouring of trust. My mother did not write a begging letter, merely one that made it clear that she knew her government would treat her with fairness and honor: not a bad point of view to encourage in an old lady who would live in a foreign country for the rest of her years.

Now the wheel has turned again, and the Coalport cups and saucers, the little spoons, and what remains of the Ready money have come to me. Of course there isn't anywhere near as much in the Ready account as there used to be, but I can still call up a genie of sorts from time to time. Last winter, for example, my husband and I had a vacation in Hawaii, and thanks to James Teversal Reading we were able to stretch our holiday to include a tour of the marvellous outer islands. During our return trip, the plane we were due to fly in to the mainland was cancelled, and we were squeezed on to a different flight. As we scurried across Honolulu airport and scrambled aboard, I thought of Ready and his London train. We were running for a jumbo jet, but in-under-the-wire the way he liked it, some ninety years after he had first fallen in love with Hester's teeth.

Anny's Men

Bonnie Raymond took over the next bed when Nona Smithson left. I didn't know it at the time, but Bonnie was to be the last of my roommates: I was to go home myself in a few days. Bonnie was a bright, cheerful woman in her forties—the mother of three sons (the youngest was attending Bethesda Chevy Chase High School) and the wife of a lawyer. The whole family had recently returned from a trip to Europe, where they had packed themselves into a small rented car and covered a great deal of territory. Bonnie was in hospital now for repairs to a broken hip incurred when she took a corner near her Washington home too fast. She was furious about it, of course, after doing her share of driving on foreign roads and in foreign traffic without any mishaps.

One of the reasons for the Raymonds' trip, apart from taking a vacation, was to visit the parents of an English boy and his sister for whom Bonnie's parents had provided a home during World War II. The English evacuee 'children' were now in their twenties—the boy was a Chartered Accountant in London and the girl a nurse. The two families had kept in touch but this was the first opportunity there had been for the British side to return some of the American hospitality that the children had enjoyed. The Raymonds had been whisked about from one social event to another and royally entertained.

I was interested in everything that Bonnie had to say (once she stopped fuming over her hip) partly because I enjoyed her comments on my native countrymen and their habits ("Now give me an honest answer—do English people really *prefer* raw bacon to cooked bacon, and cold toast to hot?") and partly because I remembered a somewhat similar case of hospitality, though in reverse. Mine concerned my Aunt Helen and some adult Americans—members of the U.S. Air Force who, during World War II, were stationed at a dreary, former Royal Air Force Base near her home.

The household, a three-bedroom apartment in the London suburb of Ealing, consisted of Aunt Helen, her maid Benson, and Benson's illegitimate daughter, Anny. My aunt had taken the apartment because when her husband died, the house in which she had lived for most of her married life felt too large. Helen spent two years methodically sorting through her possessions and deciding which to keep and which to part with, and two days selling her old home, acquiring her new one, and moving. "I can't understand why people say moving is so much trouble," she remarked to me. "The Real Estate Office had a buyer for the house and a nice empty flat right there on their books, and the van people said they'd had a cancellation, and if I could be ready by next Wednesday—'Next *Wednesday!*' I told them, 'What am I supposed to do till then? I'm ready *now.*'" The transition was made smoothly. We watched the house emptied and the furniture leave, and then we walked the three blocks between my aunt's old home and her new one. Helen carried her jewellery case, Benson carried Anny, and I carried a hat-box containing tea, milk, sugar, and a walnut cake.

My aunt's marriage had lasted more than thirty years. Her husband, Reginald Greene, whom I remembered as a tall thin man with a high forehead, sparse sandy hair, and watery blue eyes, had been a Scotland Yard detective. I am sure it helped him in his work that he gave the impression of being the kind of person who could easily be taken in: he was gentle and mild-mannered and (apparently) vague. His hobby was reading detective stories, over which he would chortle quietly whenever he caught the detective-story detective making professional mistakes.

The Greenes had no children and their life together was tidy. They both did their stints of good works in the neighborhood, serving on church committees, visiting at the hospital (Helen), and acting as sponsor of a local boys' club (Reginald). With the assistance of a resident cook and a parlormaid who came by the day, they gave frequent small dinner parties, and most weekends they went into central London together to a theatre or a concert. Reginald belonged to a coin club and Helen kept up what was, even then, an old-fashioned practice of At Home Days. On the first and third Tuesdays of every month, her friends could be sure of finding her at home in her pretty drawingroom between three and five in the afternoon, pouring tea into Minton cups and passing cucumber and patum-peperium sandwiches.

Their orderly house was delightful to visit. Helen prided herself on house-management. When one stayed in their rambling, Victorian home, one signed a flat red leather guest-book that had been in use since the Greenes' married, and their guest-room, in addition to being supplied with books, writing materials, and a basket of needles and thread, also contained a box of petitsbeurres biscuits in case one felt peckish in the night.

All the time I was a student, I had a standing invitation to Sunday lunch at the Greenes', and I often availed myself of it. As I stepped through their front door—a heavy affair with diamond-shaped panes of colored glass in the upper panels—I had the sense of stepping out of one world and into another. I recognized that the noise, crowding, and competition that I was accustomed to in the hostel where I lived were out of place here, where everything was quiet and spacious and smelled of flowers and the best furniture polish.

The atmosphere at the Greenes' was, of course, deliberate. My aunt believed that the best way she could serve her husband was to insist that he leave all his work problems at the door, and this meant that the rest of us had to do the same. I don't think she could have done this if she had been remotely interested in crime, but she wasn't. One time when I asked her if Reginald was busy solving a particularly gory murder case, accounts of which were splashed all over the front pages of the newspapers, she merely sighed and said: "Oh yes, my dear, I expect so. Your uncle has to spend a great deal of his time in the company of very unattractive people."

I took it for granted that although my life was changing all the time, the Greenes' life was settled, and that it would continue to flow along beside mine, as steadily as a river. It was a shock, therefore, when one day in 1935 Helen had a severe heart attack. The treatment for heart patients was to put them to bed for a couple of months and then on a permanent regimen of diet and rest, and the Greenes' adapted themselves quickly and sensibly to these conditions. They rearranged their house so that the room that had been the dining-room became my aunt's bedroom, and they added a downstairs bathroom and a ramp from the back hall into the garden. By the time all this was done, the cook who had been with them for years decided to retire, and the parlormaid got married. My aunt telephoned to her usual employment agency for replacements and discovered that there were none. Life was changing everywhere and there were no takers for a job in a house whose mistress was an invalid.

There was a good deal to be said for the maids' objections. The Greenes' did not live simply. They expected to be served four full meals a day, plus early morning tea, and a late-evening snack. I am sure it would not have occurred to either of them to modify this arrangement—instead, Reginald retired. With some daily cleaning help and hot luncheons delivered by a Meal Service, he kept things running as my aunt was accustomed to having them run, for over three years. During that time, when one went to call, Helen would be resting on the drawing-room sofa (in winter) or on a glider in the garden (in summer), while Reginald plodded about attending to his household duties, always a chore or two in arrears. And then, in July of 1938, he had a heart attack himself. He'd been mowing the lawn, and he stopped beside my aunt's glider and made some comment about the heat. She was about to tell him that he'd done enough and not to attempt any more that day, when he toppled over, and before the doctor could be sent for, he was dead.

My aunt treated her widowhood with calmness and composure. She and Reginald had often discussed death and separation, although naturally they had assumed that it would be Helen who would go first. A trained nurse was engaged to see my aunt through the week of the funeral, and after that a series of temporary maids came in—temporaries always seemed to be available, but they brought with them problems that couldn't or wouldn't be left outside the door. Meanwhile my aunt persevered—she advertized widely for a living-in housekeeper, but without any success.

War was in the air. There was a good deal of speculation about air-raids, and some people thought that anyone who did not have to live in a city or in the suburbs of a city should be ordered to move out into the country. Others believed that the right of every man to live where he pleased was one of the things that democracies fought wars about. My aunt ignored such talk. She disliked the English countryside and she had no intention of living there. All the same, when war did break out a year later, she knew she had to do something. She couldn't manage on her own, and the opening of a factory in the adjacent borough of Southall (short hours, good pay, and Music-While-You-Work) was rapidly drying up the flow of temporary help.

My aunt didn't complain. She realized that her difficulties were nothing compared to those that World War II was bringing to most people.

She was, however, considerably relieved when the Rector of St. Mark's, the church she attended, suggested a solution: Benson. Benson (her full name was Ann Mary Benson, but she preferred to use only her surname) was a guest at St. Mark's House, a church-supported establishment for the care of unmarried mothers and their babies. Benson was thirty-five, she liked cooking, she had no objection to a reasonable amount of housework, and she was looking for a home for herself and her child.

My aunt demurred. Benson's morals were Benson's business, but a child in the house was something else—Helen was not accustomed to children. If Benson proved satisfactory, however, Benson might stay: a woman with a child under fourteen living with her was exempt from the draft.

So my aunt agreed to meet mother and daughter. "But I don't suppose it will work," she told me. "A woman with a past is bound to want to talk about it. I've told the Rector that if Benson and I come to any kind of an arrangement, it has got to be on the understanding that we start fresh and clear, with the past pushed aside as quickly as possible and no dragging it out and *mulling* over it. All I've ever had to offer anybody is the peace and quiet of my home, and I won't let Hitler or anyone else upset that. Your uncle knew how I felt."

My aunt was a good and kind woman, but she was narrow, too. I used to think she must amuse the Almighty by the intensity with which she sang the hymn about Jesus calling her o'er the tumult of her life's wild restless sea, when she really had no first-hand experience of wild restlessness in any form—she merely knew *about* it, and that it was one of the problems that other people, out of respect to her, left outside her door.

The interview with Benson took place in the St. Mark's parlor, with the rector there to effect introductions. It went extremely well. Benson and my aunt knew within two minutes of meeting that each was what the other wanted. Helen was relieved to find that this particular un-married mother exuded reliability and strength; there was something very reassuring about Benson's homely face, quiet manner, and straight back. Benson on her side saw with relief that Mrs. Greene meant what she said. Benson was never going to be asked, nor would she ever have to explain, about her baby.

Anny was, of course, present at her mother's interview. She slept through most of it, and during the bit when she was awake, she smiled. To say that she won my aunt over would not be strictly true, but she did manage to convey the notion that far from being a drawback to the Greene household, she might be an asset: Anny, even as a tiny thing, looked exactly like her solid, reliable, ugly mother.

Most plain women have a redeeming feature or two. Benson had none. Her head was large, her mouth wide, her black eyes small and close together, and her hair, which she wore scraped back into a bun on her neck, straight and wispy. What she lacked in appearance, though, she made up in character. Benson had no affectations, no pre-tensions, and few weaknesses. She was solid as a rock.

My aunt might not wish to know Benson's story, but I did. I never had the nerve to ask about it directly, but over the years I learned that Benson came from a small town in southern England, where her father was manager of the local bank. She had taken a nursing training after she finished high school, and then switched to teaching. She loved children—all children—and the only thing she really wanted out of life was a child of her own. Who Anny's father was I never discovered—I never even heard him mentioned except for one remark let fall by Anny when she was about five years old. ("My Daddy was a Bad One. I am to do better," was what she said.) Benson's pregnancy had been—understandably, at that time—quite beyond the acceptance of her small-town banking parents, and Benson had gone to London and had coped alone.

The Greene-Benson *mènage à trois* turned out to be a very happy one, with my aunt and Benson carefully respecting each other's privacy, and Anny fitting into the household as merrily as a puppy. Helen, who until she met Anny had invariably treated babies with the caution with which one treats a can of insecticide that has become separated from its label, found it pleasant to have a little surprise injected into the orderliness of her living. She spoiled Anny almost as much as Benson did, and Anny, who was very badly brought up according to the standards of the day—she ate when she was hungry and slept when she was tired—grew and waxed strong not so much in a lonely childhood as in a warm and friendly adult world. Everywhere that Benson went, Anny went too, at first strapped to her mother's back like a papoose, and later trailing behind, holding on to Benson's skirt. The arrangement somewhat delayed the housework, but Benson had all day and my aunt, who had grown accustomed to Reginald's pottering methods, wasn't in a hurry. It would take Benson and Anny a good half hour each evening to put the drawing-room to bed, and another half hour each morning to prepare it for the day. (Putting the drawing-room to bed meant covering the furniture with dust-sheets, taking the flowers out of the room, and running a mop over the woodwork and a carpetsweeper over the rug.)

Although my aunt and Benson communicated little, it soon became Helen's practice to consult Benson before she made a major decision. It was, therefore, Benson who pointed out that when my aunt went looking for an apartment, she should insist on one with a drawing-room that faced south, since that would be where she would be spending most of her time.

The new apartment that the three of us walked around to in 1940, after we'd seen the old house emptied of its furniture (Anny was then a year old) had exactly that—whatever sun there was would strike the drawing-room. It also had a good-sized cellar which my aunt and Benson fitted up as an air-raid shelter. (Benson didn't like what she knew of rural living any better than my aunt did, and her feeling about Anny was that this war was her war too, and rather than evacuate her under one of the Government's free evacuation schemes, she wanted her to stay where she was and experience as much of what was going on around her as she was able).

Helen had not supposed that with her weak heart she could do anything in the way of war work, but one day in June of 1943 it occurred to her that she could at least offer what she had: her pretty drawing-room with its comfortable armchairs. An American Air Force Unit had recently taken over a nearby R.A.F. depot, and—after consulting Benson—my aunt wrote a letter to the American C.O., saying that she would be delighted to put her drawing-room at the disposal of the allied visitors, every afternoon from two to five. She added that although she could not, unfortunately, provide refreshments, there would be books and magazines and games and a small radio, and whenever her coal-ration permitted, a fire.

The C.O. wrote a polite reply, but for several weeks there were no callers. Then one afternoon Corporal Alan Mirfield from Winchester Center, Connecticut, and his friend Corporal Fred Walsh from Otis, Massachusetts, rang the bell. Anny, who was doorman, was delighted. It was a chilly damp day with no sun, and my aunt hadn't felt she could run to a fire that week, but the corporals stayed for nearly two hours, and when they left they gave Anny an orange and said they hoped to come again.

The corporals broke the ice. From then on, there were usually two or three visitors every day, and sometimes as many as ten. My aunt and Benson made a point of staying in the background, but Anny was always to the fore, her ugly little face puckered in smiles. Benson and my aunt tried to discourage the Americans from bringing her presents. They explained that, owing to the cleverness of Lord Woolton, the Minister of Food, Anny was getting quite as much fruit and candy as was good for her on her special Child's Ration Book, but this did not stop the flow of goodies from the States, and after a while they gave up. The Americans, it seemed, appreciated the opportunity to give of their largesse almost as much as they appreciated the opportunity to sit about in comfortable armchairs and read the English newspapers. Not all the presents went in Anny's direction, either. ("Nylon stockings, Madam! Twelve pairs. I never! That must be Sergeant Peters—him with the bad back."

"How do you know he has a bad back?"

"From the way he walks. A short man doesn't take those long strides unless his back hurts.")

Since my aunt and Benson never intruded on the drawing-room in the afternoons, they never got to know any of the Americans well. It would have been hard in any case to make friends of them individually, since they changed frequently as their tours of duty changed, although the daily numbers at the flat remained about the same. Anny couldn't tell one American from another, but she adored them all, and it was because it was so clear that that feeling was mutual that my aunt began calling the visitors Anny's men. Anny, playing checkers and snakes and ladders and snap and grandfather's whiskers day after day, was a substitute for countless little five-year-old Americans back home. Her warm, puckering grin dried up any amount of homesickness. Anny's old-fashioned manners delighted the visitors. She would curtsey as she opened the front door, and then say over and over: "Good After-noooon! Good After-noo-oon!"

It wasn't long before my aunt and Benson found themselves regarded as a responsibility of the U.S. Air Force. When a faucet needed fixing or a light switch refused to work, someone from the base would come by and put it right—no small asset for two civilian women in wartime. And then there was the night a bomb dropped at the end of my aunt's street. Anny's men were round in a flash, startling everybody with their shouting and banging. "You ladies all right in there?" they wanted to know, when my aunt and Benson and Anny peeped cautiously out. "Not scared too bad?"

"Oh yes, thank you!" my aunt replied. "How *very* kind of you to call."

The hospitality of my aunt's chilly drawing-room was never abused: my aunt was impressed with how politely and punctiliously Anny's men behaved. If cigarette ash was accidentally dropped on the carpet, Anny would be sent for the carpet-sweeper, while the last man to leave at the end of the afternoon stacked the magazines in the rack and put away the books and games.

It seemed particularly strange, therefore, when with the ending of the war and the departure of the Americans, none of Anny's men came around to say goodbye. The only way that my aunt knew they had gone was because there were no more afternoon callers. Later, Benson and Anny reported, after one of their daily walks, that the police on duty at the Air Base gate were Royal Air Force police again. Then for several Christmasses, cards came from Winchester Center, Connecticut; Otis, Massachusetts; Chamberlain, South Dakota; Lexington, Virginia; Livermore, California; and two Chicago suburbs. After that there was silence until 1956, the year Anny became seventeen.

My aunt had died in 1955—her weak heart didn't catch up with her till then. She left Benson as her sole legatee, which meant a small but adequate pension. Anny was attending a secretarial school in Ealing when the letter with the Connecticut postmark arrived. Anny's men, it seemed, had held a reunion, and it had been voted to thank my aunt for her wartime hospitality by inviting Anny to spend six weeks in America.

Anny, of course, was beside herself with excitement. To her, as to most young Europeans, America was the paradise one dreamed of (American clothes, American food, American music, American movies) and here she was in an unheard-of situation, being offered the chance to see it all for herself. She didn't remember any of the men, but she remembered their oranges and candy, and answering the door and curtseying to the visitors, and the games of snakes and ladders and grandfather's whiskers, and the way one could watch one's breath float in the air on the days when my aunt's coal ration wouldn't run to a drawing-room fire. She even remembered the bomb at the end of the road, and the way her men had come over from the base to make sure they were all right. As she pointed out to Benson, the invitation couldn't have come at a better time. Her secretarial course was just ending, and she hadn't begun looking for a job. If she were ever to indulge in a six-week vacation, now was the opportunity. Anny accepted by return mail.

The trip was an immense success. Anny's men and their wives planned such a splendid tour that it almost seemed as if they were competing with each other as to who could give her the most fun. She saw Yosemite and the Grand Canyon and the Bad Lands and the Black Hills, and New York and Washington and San Francisco and Chicago. One of her hosts was a forester, another worked in an automobile plant, another helped his father in a country general store, another had his own restaurant. Two had built their own homes, a third had an apartment high up in a skyscraper, another had a cabin at the edge of a lake. Anny was taken camping and picnicking and square-dancing and to a night-club in a cellar, and she learned to eat hot dogs and hamburgers and enormous plates of ice-cream. Anny's men thought of everything. In addition to bus and train and airline tickets, they gave her pocket-money, and even unfilled spots on her itinerary for her to use in whatever ways she felt inclined.

America and Americans lived up to, or exceeded, Anny's dreams. The trip had been given to her as a means of thanking Helen Greene, but sometimes when thanks are expressed as circuitously as these had to be, they take over and take root. This is what seems to have happened at the inn on the Great West Road in England between Heathrow Airport and London, where Anny, Benson, Anny's husband, and Anny's young son make their home. The inn isn't what one usually thinks of as an English inn—rustic, dark, and smelling of beer, with Cornish pasty on the counter. It is large and light and modern, with traffic streaming past the door. There are three bars and a dining-room and a place out back that can be rented for banquets. Anny's husband is big, solid, industrious, and popular. It is clear that Anny has indeed done better with her man than Benson did with the Bad One.

The last time I saw Anny, which was a few years ago, I thought she looked fine. She wasn't any handsomer than she had ever been, but she still had old-fashioned manners, and about certain things she was severe. "I don't hold with any anti-American feeling here," she told me. "The regulars know that, but now and again we get one in from the airport, and if their attitude ain't right, I tell them to leave—and they do. We've never had any fuss. We always fly the stars and stripes on Independence Day. Eric says he isn't sure it's proper, but I say if anyone objects, send him to *me.*"

Benson lives upstairs, in two large rooms that get whatever sun reaches *The Red Lion.* She reads, and sews, and baby-sits for her grandson, spoiling him just the way she spoiled his mother. She admits that the Great West Road is noisy (on Saturday nights a rock band tunes up downstairs) but she combats this with earplugs, and a large television set.

I wonder sometimes if Benson ever thinks about the Bad One, and whether it surprises her that her daughter has never, apparently, been curious about her origins. The Bad One could walk into one of the bars at any time—I feel that of the three it would be the classiest, the Saloon Bar, that he would choose—and buy a pint of bitter from Anny without, of course, having any idea who she was. If he stayed around long enough, or if he dropped in on the Fourth of July, he would soon discover the fierce little candle of pro-American sentiment that the innkeeper's wife keeps burning there, but he has been left outside the door too long himself, poor fellow, for it to be possible for him to understand what has been going on, or to appreciate the warm alive thing that was planted in Anny by Helen Greene's timid war effort, and watered by the gratitude of Anny's men.

Erika

By the time we got back to America, we were feeling really well. Charles still had trouble eating thick sandwiches, and I suppose he always will, just as I shall always have a certain mushiness in my speech. (I sound as if I have just fortified myself with slightly more alcohol than is wise.) We have learned to see the whole experience of our crash in more reasonable perspective, though. At the start, my entire energy and attention were required either to take in a breath of air or expel it, and the notion that other people might not be as deeply concerned with this activity of mine as I seemed wholly unrealistic. Then gradually I became aware that life existed not only beyond the end of my bed, but beyond the next bed also, and even beyond the walls of Hill Hospital. For months after I had learned to talk again, I described our accident eagerly to anybody I could persuade to listen. I prattled (gratefully and slurringly) about the attention we had received from so many quarters, and I told of the middle-aged negro who shared Charles's room for a time and who appeared to be quite alone in the world, with neither visitors, flowers, telephone calls, get-well cards, nor bedroom slippers. (Whenever he became aware that Charles needed assistance, he would run over on his long bare feet, smiling and eager to know what he could do.) I boasted about us, finding it hard to believe that we could have been more badly damaged than we were and still return to normal living. What I didn't realize, at least not until I renewed acquaintance (briefly) with Erika, was how much we owed our recovery to one small fact. When we were hurt, we were grown adults: not children.

I met Erika (and Erika's sloth) quite by chance one Saturday morning in Washington, D.C. It was the winter after our accident, and I was now able to widen my thinking enough to appreciate other people's aches and pains instead of only my own. I had gone across town to a different section of the city from the one in which we live, to take flowers to an office colleague of Charles's who was sick. I had known Erika years before in London, and I knew where in Washington she lived because one of my cousins had sent me her address. I hadn't looked her up, though. I hadn't thought she would want me to, and I think I was right.

Erika had come to England from Germany in 1937, under an adoption scheme sponsored by the Red Cross. She was eight years old then, and her background was a sad one. She was an only child, and both her parents had been killed in a street riot in Heidelberg; her father had been a professor in the science school of the university there. The English couple who adopted Erika were next-door neighbors of my aunt Helen in Ealing. Their name was Bullen. Peter Bullen worked at the Home Office, and he and his wife, Edith, were very active in local community affairs—the Ealing hospital, the Y, and so on. They were both cheerful, generous people, and part of the reason they offered Erika a home, I think, was that their own two daughters were grown and married, and they wanted to have someone young around the house again.

It took nearly a year before all the formalities connected with the adoption were completed, and during that time Erika waited in a Heidelberg orphanage. The Bullens wrote frequently and sent snapshots of themselves and the Ealing house and garden, their daughters, their daughters' husbands and the one grandchild, their overfed spaniel, Crumpet, and their three cats. Erika responded with neatly written letters in stilted, correct English and, after being pressured for it, a photograph, faded, showing a thin little girl with a long face, large eyes, and shoulder-length, straight black hair. She was not a pretty child. Her eyes were her best feature; she had one of those short upper lips that expose the front teeth and give the face a wary, ferrety look.

When the time came for the Bullens to take delivery of Erika (they met her at Waterloo Station and signed for her at the Red Cross office) they realized at once that the snapshot was a good likeness. Erika's personality fitted her picture: she was graven, obedient, watchful, and aloof. The Bullens consoled themselves with the thought that once established in Ealing and fed Edith's cooking for a few weeks Erika would fill out and relax and soon become as loving, outgoing, and delightful as their own children had been. They were mistaken. But they had done some conscientious reading, and they knew that it is possible for affection to be damaged and retarded and that they must give Erika time. What was hard on them, and especially hard on the warmhearted, demonstrative Edith, was that the Red Cross never told them—if, indeed, the Red Cross knew—exactly what the destructive circumstances in Erika's life had been. All they knew was that the silent child who had joined their family was alive in a quite different way from themselves.

The Bullens persevered. They corralled their neighbors, including my aunt, to help settle Erika in. I was a student at London University at the time, and as I often went to Sunday lunch in Ealing, I was corralled also. One Sunday it was suggested that I introduce Erika to the London Zoo. I wasn't keen. Erika to date hadn't shown any interest in animals—she avoided fat Crumpet and the cats, and when Peter said something about buying her a puppy of her own she had merely looked alarmed. However, the proposal made better sense than it sounds because my parents were members of the London Zoological Society, and at that time (I don't know what the regulations are now) this meant that if the keepers weren't busy one could sometimes go behind the scenes and handle the animals.

It takes about an hour to go by bus from Ealing to Regent's Park where the zoo is, and Erika and I made the journey in almost complete silence. She wasn't a child that I took to, and I had growing-up problems of my own to occupy my mind. The visit wasn't a complete failure, though. Erika seemed to be fascinated. Moving slowly from cage to cage, she subjected whatever was living on the other side of the bars or wire or glass to the closest scrutiny. At one point, a keeper asked if the little lady would like to tickle a sloth behind its ear. The little lady shook her head, so the cage was unlocked for me and I did the tickling.

After that, Erika and I went to the zoo quite often. We never became what you could call communicative, but we did have our visits to the zoo as one point of contact, and Erika got to where she would occasionally agree to touch or hold an animal. I remember waiting nearly an hour one damp Sunday while Erika helped a keeper feed a jar of apple custard to a very small and shy chimpanzee.

Erika had arrived in England in May, and the following September the Bullens put her in school. They chose a large place with a high academic reputation, where foreign-born students were encouraged, thinking that Erika would feel less conspicuous there and find it easier to make friends than at the small school to which they had sent their own daughters. They were mistaken again. Erika made herself conspicuous at once by moving to the top of her class and remaining there, and she neither made nor seemed to want to make any friends.

I don't remember when it was that Erika and I lost touch, but our zoo trips had stopped before I finished at the university. Thereafter I only had news of her at long intervals. From her London school she went on to Cambridge, and then to America as a Henry Fellow. She got a Ph.D in Zoology from Yale.

After Charles and I were married and I had been living in Washington for several years, one of my English cousins wrote to say that Erika was working nearby: she had a job with the Smithsonian Institution. I was curious to see her again, but in view of our past relationship I thought I would leave it to her to make the first move—she had been given our address, my cousin said. I gathered that Erika hadn't changed much. "Do see what you can do to persuade her to write to those poor Bullens," my cousin wrote. "They're so proud of what she's done with herself, and they really know nothing about her life."

I wondered if I would recognize Erika if I saw her again, but when I did I knew her at once. We ran into each other on Capitol Hill outside her apartment house—I coming out after delivering my plant, and she going in. She looked exactly as I would have expected her to look at thirty-five: neat, capable, unassuming, and remote. She wore a black suit, a white blouse, low-heeled walking shoes, and a shoulder bag that left her hands free for carrying two big bags of groceries. She hesitated when she saw me, then recovered herself and smiled as I took one of the grocery bags. "I'm afraid I'm on the third floor," she said.

It was an old building, a Victorian house that had been converted, and we climbed the stairs. We didn't talk (picking up just where we had left off, I thought), and I decided that even if Erika asked me to I wouldn't turn this into a visit—I would put the groceries down and leave.

I didn't quite manage that, though I don't think I was in the apartment for more than five minutes. What delayed me was the sight of a sloth. I saw him the moment she unlocked her front door; the door into her bedroom was standing open, and there he was, suspended from the bottom rail of her metal bedstead, fast asleep.

The front door opened into the living room, and now I noticed two other animals. Each was in a small crate with a chicken-wire front. One was a golden marmoset and the other was what I took to be a porcupine (it was lying down). The room, sparsely furnished and spotlessly clean, was very warm and had a faint odor of antiseptic. As we walked across it—the kitchen was at the far end—I saw that the marmoset's tail was in a white cast about the diameter of a cigarette, though longer. The creature's leonine face was puckered with rage. It clung desperately to the wire netting with its hooked claws, as if it were in pain and the netting were life. The echidna—that's what the other animal was, Erika explained, not a porcupine—merely lay with its eyes closed, seeming to be waiting for whatever was hurting it to go away.

Before she unpacked the groceries or took any further notice of me, Erika attended to her patients. She didn't open their cages or speak to them—just stood close to them, as one might stand beside a hospital bed, offering the occupant one's silence when all that can be done has been done. The marmoset chattered and rattled his wire, his eyes fiercely alert and his minute fangs bared. The echidna neither opened its eyes nor moved, and presently Erika came back into the kitchen and began putting her food away.

I am sure that if I had left the apartment then she wouldn't have been aware of the fact. Her face wore the same brooding look of concentration that I remembered from Regent's Park. But I had to know what she was doing, and so, for the first time since I had known her, I asked questions. She explained that her department at the Smithsonian was the National Zoo, where she had charge of the smaller sick or abandoned animals. During the week, she kept them in a hospital on the zoo grounds, but on the weekends she brought them home with her; the landlord hadn't approved at first, but she had satisfied him that her patients would not cause any trouble, that he would not know they were there. But what about the sloth, I asked? He wasn't sick, was he?

Well, no. The sloth wasn't sick. He had been abandoned by his mother at birth. After his first weekend on the bedrail, he had seemed so comfortable that the director had said he might stay temporarily, and now, Erika hoped, he had been forgotten. Peering at me, she added the information that the creature was no problem: sloths urinated only once a week.

Did he ever do anything except sleep on the bedrail, I asked. Did he know her? Yes, indeed, Erika assured me. He not only knew her, but he could tell the time. Every day at five, he moved from the bedrail to the handle of the front door. When she came home and turned the handle, the sloth fell off and awoke. That way he knew she was home.

I took my leave then. Neither Erika nor I proposed another meeting, but the next day I wrote to the Bullens. I told them about running into Erika and everything I had learned of the work she was doing, and I hope I made her sound as useful and valuable a member of the Smith-sonian staff as I am sure she was. I described her apartment and enlarged my brief stop into a more considerable visit. I stressed the fact that her responsibilities involved her evenings as well as her days. I didn't say anything about the sloth, though. I tried, but I didn't know how to convey to jocund, ebullient Edith that Erika had found a relationship with demands so slight that she needn't be afraid of them: a fragile, barely expressed, tentative association for which even the word "velle-ity" seemed too dramatic. I wanted her to understand that Erika's ne-glect of them did not stem from a lack of regard but was simply the result of a wound—a sense of abandonment—so acute that it had never properly healed.

Edith replied to my letter by return mail. She and Peter felt so reas-sured. They could now believe and tell their friends what they wanted to believe and tell their friends: that Erika was successful, happy, val-ued, and busy—too busy, in fact, to write.

For me, that wasn't the whole story. Seeing Erika again had been a sobering experience. I understood very well what it meant to be damaged—I had been talking of little else since I relearned to speak. But my damage was physical, and it happened when I was an adult and not a child. Unlike Erika, I had been able to defend myself. I was old enough and grown enough to fight back. And survive.

Hill Climbing by Boat

Charles and I promised ourselves a vacation as soon as we were free of hospitals, speech-therapy sessions, and law-suits (we sued the drunk driver who hit us, and although we lost our case the first time around, we won it on appeal). It was, however, several months before we felt sufficiently ambitious to do more than talk about a trip—where we would go and what we would do. Usually we plan holidays that will provide us with plenty of outdoor exercise, but this time we were bent on inactivity. We both like to travel by water (the first time we went to England together, we arrived in the Pool of London by boat, stern first), and we don't mind too much about a lack of warmth and sunshine. In the end, we settled for a very very slow cruise. If we had cruised any more slowly than we did, I think we wouldn't have moved at all. We became two of the twelve passengers carried by the *Nora*, as she covered (in a week) approximately seventy miles of England's inland waterways.

We joined the *Nora* at Braunston Junction, a village fifteen miles south of Rugby, Warwickshire, on the Coventry Canal. The *Nora* was a canal narrow-boat built in 1930 to carry coal, and later converted to passenger use. She was, and may still be, for all I know, one of several holiday craft that plied the inland waterways of England during the summer months. At least four private companies, operating, so far as we were able to ascertain, one pair of boats apiece, organized one- and two-week cruises. Their passengers lived, slept, and ate on board.

By canal tradition, narrow-boats travel in pairs: our leader (the *Nora*) contained a diesel and towed an engineless "butty" (the *Mendip*). The *Nora* was seventy-two feet long and drew five feet. Built as a horse-drawn craft, she could carry twenty-five tons of coal in her open hold, astern of which were the diesel and her skipper's living quarters. She belonged to two young architects, Peter and Janet Turton, who called themselves the Onshore Waterways. They designed the remodeled passenger-carrying *Nora*, doing much of the actual rebuilding themselves. They gave *Nora* a well deck, a saloon, and four tiny cabins, each fitted with electric light and running hot and cold fresh water. (A sign on our cabin window said "Please do not climb out.") The *Mendip*, lacking an engine, rode higher in the water than the *Nora*, so that her roof was the best place to watch whatever was going on—provided one did not forget to lie down flat at a bridge approach (frightful accidents, including decapitation, could occur if one failed to do so). The *Mendip* included a well deck, three double cabins, a dining saloon, and a galley. Six passengers traveled in each boat, a crew of four was distributed between them, and Amanda, a handsome Dalmatian owned by the mate, shared quarters with the engine.

Charles and I had expected that our skipper Peter Turton and his crew would be middle-aged, and the passengers young. In fact, it turned out to be rather the other way around. Sailing with us were a retired army man and his wife, a librarian and his family, a department-store buyer, two students, and two nurses. (One of the nurses, a city girl, found the casualness of life in rural Warwickshire shocking. "Don't they leave the sheep out *late!*" she exclaimed.) As for the crew, it was composed of three lively and highly competent young women, all of whom appeared to share Peter Turton's eagerness to work from dawn to dark seven days a week from May to October, and rather longer during the rest of the year, when repairs, repainting, and planning must be done. Neither did any of the crew seem to mind what kind of work she or he did. There can be few passenger vessels afloat in which the skipper and mate not only navigate, but also wash dishes, polish brassware and scrub decks.

This attitude to work—as if it were nothing but pleasure—becomes perfectly understandable once one is actually travelling on the "cut" as a canal is called. Once you are aboard, you feel as if you are in a different element, where time seems more a matter of deliberate leisure than deliberate speed.

We had not supposed that on so narrow a waterway, we would be treated the way people the world over are treated the moment it is observed that they are waterborne, but we were. Everyone was our friend. Dour persons disconsolately fishing and forced to withdraw their lines from the water as we crept by, ceased to be dour and smiled. (One had more than a dozen roach, mostly six to eight inches long. He used boiled hempseed for bait.) Tiny cars high up on bridges blocked traffic while their occupants wound their windows down to wave. Children ran down cottage-garden paths to where they could be closer to the magic that was ourselves. On the edge of a small town, we passed behind a dowdy-looking factory. Suddenly the dirty windows were filled with girls' faces. "What do you do in there?" we asked. "Make pretty hats!" they cried.

A narrow-boat holiday is not a holiday for anyone with a weight problem. We ate excellently, six times a day: early morning tea, breakfast, mid-morning coffee, luncheon, afternoon tea, and dinner; there was also a fully equipped bar at which, oddly, one purchased one's breakfast fruit juice. Nor was it cheap. English friends were horrified when we told them that our week on the *Nora*—the tariff included everything except drinks—had cost us some 90 pounds apiece. It was the Turtons' opinion, however, that they must provide the meals and services of a first-class hotel if they were to attract the kind of passengers they wanted, i.e. people who would find leisure sufficiently rewarding in itself, without the added charms of organized entertainment. "People who come looking for a dance band on deck are out of luck," Peter said.

Most narrow boats do not provide the *Nora*'s and *Mendip*'s high standard of comfort. Canal folk who carry coal and timber still live much the way they did in the eighteenth century, sleeping, eating, and raising families in cabins twelve feet long and seven feet wide. One family we met told us, amid giggles, of a problem on board another pair of boats that housed father, mother, and seven little children. Next week five older brothers and sisters, now boarding at a Canal Children's Hostel in London, were due home for the summer holidays, and there would be fourteen to sleep in the two twelve-foot cabins, one partly filled by the diesel.

Most canal people are the descendants of canal people—a boatman isn't usually able to persuade a shore-raised girl to marry him. Few canal men can read or write, but they want their children to learn, and families are willing to separate so that their youngsters can live at special hostels from which they attend school. The children do not like coming off the water any better than their parents do (one retired narrow-boatman makes his home in a double-decker London bus parked on the canal bank, where the view is familiar and the quarters must seem palatial). Canal children's hostels do, however, have their compensations: a bed to oneself, for example, and different clothes to wear at night from those one wears in the daytime.

Everyone old enough to do so helps with the work. One job that frequently seemed to fall to a young member of a family was cycling along the towpath of the "pound", the stretch of water between two locks, and preparing the lock that lay ahead. The tool for this operation is known as a windlass, and when not in use the bicycle boy wore it neatly tucked into the belt of his trousers.

Locks mostly run in series, a group of three or four together, although some are actually in steps, the top gate of one acting as the bottom gate of another. We watched one coal-boat skipper and his wife towing a butty: there seemed to be a knack about towing, a little like that of a bellringer ringing a heavy bell—the pull on the rope was not so much a matter of strength as of timing and steadiness. The couple we saw leaned heavily against the towrope, their bodies at a steep angle to the ground. They walked very close to each other, the woman behind the man, their steps tiny, measured, and graceful, as if they were treading a slow-motion ballet in time with the spring of the stretched rope.

Cranking up lock paddles is also a matter of knack. I couldn't move them at all, but quite small boys off the coal-boats seemed to have no trouble. Sometimes children are allowed to manoeuvre the boats, an operation not as simple as it sounds. At bends in the waterway, a pair of boats needs the entire width of the canal, and where approaches are blind, the skipper warns of his presence by blowing on a small, asthmatic-sounding huntsman's horn.

One surprising element of the canal world is how clean everybody manages to be. As soon as a canal-boat ties up for the night, cleaning and scrubbing usually begins. Decks and cabin roofs are swabbed down, brass fitments are polished to a shine, and spotless socks and shirts are hung to dry above, though not very far above, the precious black cargo.

Canal folk love bright colors, perhaps because most of the scenery they live in is misty and gray and softened. The narrow-boat's hull is painted black, but the tiller, the cabin, and the posts that support the tarpaulins that cover the hold in wet weather are ultramarine, crimson, pink, green, and white. These items are further decorated with leaves and flowers, especially roses, and with fairy-tale castles said to have been introduced on the canals by immigrant Carpathian gypsies. Painting these flowers and castles is the one remaining English folk art. It is quite quick for an expert to do—a kind of painter's shorthand. The main design is painted in, and individual flourishes are added after the first part is almost dry. The boatman's devotion to flowers and castles is understandable: few canal men are ever likely to own a garden, or a house that has too much space.

The *Nora*'s crew were careful to see that our boats did not interfere in any way with commercial traffic. Time is money to a coal boat, and a delay at locks may mean arrival at a destination too late to unload cargo that night, or even that weekend. There is considerable competition between one canal family and the next, each trying to make the better time. Feuds have been started by a boatman rash enough to pole past a sleeping rival in the night in an effort to beat him to the next series of locks.

As late as the sixties, there were still a few horse-drawn craft on the canals, and the marks of the old horse-traffic years were everywhere. The abutments of the arched bridges have grooves half an inch deep worn by the tow-ropes, even in places where an iron-shod guard has been added. At some of the locks there were little foot-bridges across the water just below the bottom gates, each consisting of two parts cantilevered out from the banks so that the boats' tow-ropes could slip between. A sign outside an inn read: "Licensed to sell Beer, Wine, Spirits, Music, and Singing. Good Accommodation for boat horses. Straw Provided."

A canal boat pushes water ahead of her, and if the cut is silted up or choked with weeds the water level may be affected for as much as a mile. Opposite *Nora*'s stern two inches of mossy concrete showed on the bank, but at her bows the concrete was wet for an inch above the moss. Thus we were continuously climbing a hill of three inches in every seventy feet. Try to go faster, and all that happens is that the propeller pulls water out from under the stern—a canal boat must move *past* the water in the canal, not drive it ahead.

Only the first part of *Nora*'s route was through commercially traveled and well-kept-up canals; the rest lay along neglected waterways almost unknown except to boatmen. Charles and I had supposed that we would find central England over-populated, with dormitory towns and housing projects stretching from one historic shrine to the next. But morning after morning we awoke to a remote world—those lush meadows and dark woodlands Constable was so fond of painting. One may think of canals as straight thoroughfares, but many English canals wind as much as rivers—the early navigators worked around obstacles, rather than through or over them, whenever they could. On several mornings I went walking along the meandering, little-used towpaths overgrown with wild rhubarb and old-fashioned flowers—gooseberry pudding, ladies' bedstraw, meadow crane's bill. It was easy to keep ahead of the *Nora*— her average daily run was about ten miles, and for hours I saw no sign of her. When I felt I had fought the swampy ground long enough, I would climb up on a bridge and wait for the boats. Ten or fifteen minutes before the *Nora* and *Mendip* reached me, I would usually see them, apparently moving across the middle of a distant green field. The *Nora* would swing close to the towpath at my bridge, her engine coughing politely, and I would step back on board as she passed.

The diesel made very little noise, and our progress was so quiet that we were often almost on top of the coot, swans, and diving water-rats before we disturbed them. Off a moorhen would bustle, her head jerking rhythmically back and forth. A plant we took to be water-arum seemed to curtsey to us as the *Nora*'s wash rose and fell on the stalks.

Just as fascinating, I think, as the natural scenery of the canals (and the place names: Stewpony Wharf, Sheepwash Staunch, Pluck's Gutter, Bumble-hole Bridge) was the solid and solemn beauty of the architecture. The builders of the canals had strictly utilitarian aims. Their aqueducts and bridges, tunnels, ramps, and steps were made not to look at but to work with and to last. Most of the bridges we passed under are made of brick, now well covered with gray or gray-blue lichen. As the brick weathers and crumbles, patches of lichen are carried away, and the warm red shows through. Even the inns, erected for the comfort of the early navigators, are out of this same austere and satisfying mold.

Our voyage ended at the little town of Stone, in Staffordshire. We came ashore feeling over-fed, under-washed, completely rested, and in that euphoric state in which one might well be wearing, instead of walking shoes, a small puffy cloud on each foot. (When I remarked on this to Charles, he said *his* walking shoes felt different, too—they had been put away wet under his bunk, and their soles now had a thin coating of mold.)

For nostalgic reasons, we returned (by train) to Rugby for a couple of nights. During World War II, Charles had been stationed just outside the town for nine weeks, at a beautiful house named Newbold Revel which had been commandeered for the duration by the R.A.F. He and I had met at Newbold (in different and better days, my aunts had gone to parties there), and the day after our canal trip finished, we rented a car and drove out to the house. We found that it had been turned into a school. A fluttery nun answered the doorbell when we rang, and when we asked if we might take another look at the handsome ballroom where we had first set eyes on each other (it was an Officers' Mess then), she said she did not think she could admit us to the house without the permission of the Mother Superior, and the Mother Superior was away somewhere on a Retreat.

I felt mildly irritated with the nun for not admitting us on such an auspicious occasion, but I suppose she had her orders and one could hardly blame her for keeping to them. What I really wanted to do was to convey to Charles how important this part of the world was to me, with its quaint and funny rituals and its emphasis on and respect for our black jewellery: coal.

It was several years before we visited England again, and when we did, we found (unromantically) that we remembered very little about

Newbold Revel. Instead, what remained in our minds was the coal country itself and its lacework of canals. We still talk about that trip and the remarkable work of eighteenth-century engineers who nudged boats across roads, rivers, and bridges, made them disappear into the sides of hills, and go uphill as we had done.

Joyce Warren was born in Birmingham, England, and educated at St. Selix School and tutored privately. Her first novel, OUR GLAD, was published by Harper & Row in 1957, with the aid of a grant from the Eugene Saxton Memorial Trust. PEACOCKS AND AVARICE also appeared in 1957 with Harper & Row and was translated into Finnish in the same year. GLAD TIDINGS, Harper & Row, followed in 1960. Joyce Warren has also been a dance critic for the *Washington Star*, She lives in Washington, D.C., with her husband.

The people believed that on that evening and night [the second of May] the witches were abroad and busy casting spells on cattle and stealing cows' milk. To counteract their machinations, pieces of rowan-tree and woodbine, but especially of rowan-tree, were placed over the doors of the cowhouses, and fires were kindled by every farmer and cottar.

THE GOLDEN BOUGH, James Frazer

The text of this book was set in Goudy Old Style by Graphic Composition, Athens, Georgia, and printed on acid-free paper by Malloy Lithographing, Inc., Ann Arbor, Michigan.

Rowan Tree Press
124 Chestnut Street
Boston, Massachusetts 02108